ALSO BY

SHIRLEY ANN GRAU

The Black Prince and Other Stories (1955)

The Hard Blue Sky (1958)

The House on Coliseum Street (1961)

The Keepers of the House (1964)

The Condor Passes (1971)

The Wind Shifting West (1973)

THESE ARE BORZOI BOOKS,

PUBLISHED IN NEW YORK

BY ALFRED A. KNOPF

EVIDENCE OF LOVE

EVIDENCE OF LOVE

Shirley Ann Grau

ALFRED A. KNOPF

NEW YORK

1977

c, 3

T H I S   I S   A   B O R Z O I   B O O K

P U B L I S H E D   B Y   A L F R E D   A .   K N O P F ,   I N C .

Copyright © 1977 by Shirley Ann Grau

All rights reserved under International and

Pan-American Copyright Conventions.

Published in the United States by Alfred A. Knopf, Inc., New York, and

simultaneously in Canada by Random House of Canada Limited, Toronto.

Distributed by Random House, Inc., New York.

Library of Congress Cataloging in Publication Data

Grau, Shirley Ann. / Evidence of love. / I. Title.

PZ4.G775Ev3   [PS3557.R283]   813'.5'4   76–47920

ISBN 0–394–41115–3

A limited edition of this book has been privately printed.

Manufactured in the United States of America

Published February 26, 1977

Second Printing, April 1977

James, with love

. . . I pursued,

And still pursue, the origin and course

Of love, but until now I never knew

That fluttering things have so distinct a shade.

—*Wallace Stevens, "Le Monocle de Mon Oncle"*

EDWARD

MILTON

HENLEY

Three generations of the Henley family examine their own and each other's lives for evidences of love; a search which leads the youngest to the grandmother who bore his father for money rather than emotion.

¶ I, Edward Milton Henley, was born Saturday, May 26, 1883, in the front bedroom of my family's five-storied brick townhouse. Spring that year came very early and was unseasonably warm, making my mother extremely uncomfortable. My father escaped her noisy irritability by moving to his club. From there, each morning, he sent his valet to inquire about her health and her progress toward bearing his child.

It was an eminently practical plan, enabling him to receive the latest news without the latest unpleasantness. The valet (a clever man who subsequently became a very successful merchant) simply failed to repeat any querulous or quarrelsome remarks by my mother. My father maintained his dignity even in the face of something as distasteful as childbirth.

Months earlier, my sister Caroline, who was then five, had been absorbed into my grandmother's large household in Philadelphia.

My mother and the unborn I waited alone in the heat of May. On the morning of the twenty-sixth, she sent a particularly shrewish and angry message to my father—even the estimable valet was not able to extract the venom from it. My father was, of course, quite upset. In a conciliatory spirit he sent her a huge basket of magnificent strawberries. Superb big berries, from the south somewhere, lush and bloody in their ripeness.

Apparently my mother also was ripe. One glance at those strawberries and she began her labor. She was assisted by two midwives, yellow-bonneted and white-aproned in the manner of the times, and by her own personal maid Hilda, who had attended her since girlhood and who was prepared to usher her into this second crisis of her womanhood as ceremonially as she had laced her into her bridal gown.

And the doctor. Oh yes, we had a doctor. My family were very advanced in their thinking. His name was Parker Rifkin, and he was a very learned man from Johns Hopkins. If there were any female problems (as my father said with a snicker of embarrassment), wife and child would be well cared for.

These then, maid, doctor, and midwives, waited to relieve my mother's body of my distending presence.

I have thought—I have often thought—that I can indeed remember the moment of my birth. I can hear the slosh of the waters and feel the intense enveloping compression.

I was a very annoying infant because I refused to be born head first. The doctor's hands tumbled me over, head down, properly. Deliberately I reversed myself. Ass first I would go into the world.

While the gaslights hissed and whistled softly and my body shook with my mother's straining, the hands tumbled me over again. A great wave crest carried me along, through the surf, pulsing, falling into the air. And I who had lived so comfortably under water all these months gasped and struggled with the smothering air. Like a landed fish.

Out of my element, I strangled. Panicked. Screamed.

The sound of the waters lessened and the sense of smothering ceased. I struggled successfully against the terrifying air.

I emerged from my birth aching and frightened. Years later I dreamt about it just that way, the terror and pressure and tumbling waters. I woke trembling and whimpering.

But no matter. The fact is that I was dragged forth into a mahogany-paneled room lined with Thomas Hovenden portraits and gentle pastoral scenes of the Hudson Valley and the Scottish crags, of thatched villages by tiny streams—a dignified room suddenly smelling of sweat and feces and ammonia, like any stable.

Passed among eight eager hands, I drew my early hesitant breaths in Mother's Room. (Father's Room, adjoining of course, was very much the same. Except for the pictures. His were all of animals—noble stags at bay, highly intelligent-looking dogs, impossibly muscled horses. There was also a difference in the carpets—Mother's Aubusson was considered feminine and Father's Bokhara masculine—who knows why.)

I was immediately washed in a basin of cold water, as all the children in my mother's family had been washed for three generations. The sharp dash of cold after the warm waters of the womb was supposed to promote hardiness and vigor.

(I still have that basin. Porcelain, with a rather ugly navy and gold Imari pattern. I keep it on the third-from-the-top bookshelf of my office. And yes, my office always has bookshelves. In fact, my offices are always exactly alike. Why? Because it pleases me to have it so. No other reason. I have had to move from time to time—buildings deteriorate, states and counties become less than friendly in their tax structure. But my private office remains unchanged. My manager sees to that. He himself transports my bowl in his arms from place to place.)

As a newborn I found that plunge into the cold porcelain most invigorating. I screamed constantly and made such violent demands on my mother's nipples that within a few days she turned me over to a wet nurse, who was paid to put up with my peremptory chewing habits.

As I emerged from my first bath, my mother listened to

my angry birdlike cries and she said to the midwives who were still attending her (the doctor was busy with me): "Thank heavens, it's a boy. Now I shall never have to do that again."

While the gaslights hissed their constant faint sound, the women clucked their sympathy, and the birth proceeded without incident.

Much later that evening, when all was secure, the doctor himself went to bring the news to my father, who was then busy at cards.

"A boy, splendid," my father said. "As soon as I finish this hand, we shall have a drink."

And so they did. To my mother's annoyance the doctor did not return to her house. He stayed drinking with my father and slept that night at the club. Only the carriage came home, empty except for a message from my father: "Tell my wife I shall call on her tomorrow."

And so he did. Bringing her the present he'd kept secret lest the birth be a failure—a diamond tiara that women of those days wore in their upswept hair.

The obvious expense of the diamonds softened her feelings toward him—she was most civil when he arrived—but the memory of the difficult birth proved stronger. She never received him in her bed again. She had been perfectly and literally serious when she told the midwives never again.

My father was not unduly upset by this change. Two pregnancies with a gentle wife turned irrational termagant had been quite enough for him. As for his sex life, he could easily provide for that elsewhere. I rather imagine he took a mistress or two, but no echo of them ever reached our ears. We, his wife and children, committed ourselves to the idea that Papa led a monastic life. And to tell the truth, he was, I think, a man for whom the sexual experience was of small importance. He thoroughly enjoyed the company of men; he was far more content at his club than he ever was within the confines of his family.

Of course he remained on very good terms with my mother. They understood each other completely. She had produced a son and a daughter: in the immemorial manner of women she had risked her life to please him with their births. When— months later—they formally sallied forth to church for my christening, I am sure that my father beamed upon my mother. Sincerely.

In later years, I remember them: my mother bejeweled, my father top-hatted, both totally satisfied. They were a very handsome couple, a bit portly like aging animals, but still sleek, with the air of all thoroughbreds. They regarded each other exactly the way they regarded their animals or their houses. Each saw the other as a prize possession, an object whose value far exceeded its size. A perfect diamond, to cherish and protect.

She no longer filled his bed, but she filled his life. Perhaps that is not affection or love, but it is a recognition of value. And it is very durable, very durable indeed. Because it is based on a sense of propriety.

Perhaps too that is why my marriages never succeeded. I was born completely without any sense of propriety. Any at all.

¶ Though I remember the day of my birth, I remember nothing at all of my christening. One would expect that such a splendid ecclesiastical occasion would leave some memory residue, but it did not. I know that it was middle September.

My parents had waited until the hot summer was past; in those days babies were thought to be very fragile things easily upset by changes of air. (Why they thought that anything built to withstand the human birth process could be delicate, I do not know.) And so, on one of those bright fall days filled with a golden Italian light, light that seems to rise upwards rather than fall from the sky, I was launched into the formal seas of Christianity.

My father must have been moved far beyond his usual stoical dignity. On the very day of my christening, he transferred to my name half the family railroad interests. It was evidence of his love for me, a splendid gesture, a regal gesture to welcome a newborn. He, dear man, could not possibly have foreseen the sad fate of those railroads in the approaching century. But long before that dismal end, I had sold out completely.

I've been told that there was a large and very proper reception after my christening, that our narrow street was completely jammed with carriages. Later that evening there was a not at all proper celebration among the large staff of Irish servants. My father's generosity had reached even to them, they all had cash presents, and there were many kegs of beer and even whiskey in the servants' wing of the house. There were a couple of fiddlers too, and a great deal of singing and laughing. It went on far into the night, long after my parents and I had retired to our decorous beds.

We were, I am sure, all very happy.

¶ Their celebrations completed, my parents left me, half-forgotten, to endure through the ten years of my childhood.

I remember mostly boredom, and the annoyance of living

in a world where everything was too large. I remember the undersides of tables and being able to stand upright under the great hanging cloths, hiding while my nurse searched frantically for me. I also remember an endless series of nurses, all of them, absolutely all of them, smelling alike. I suppose it must have been the starch the laundress used.

I remember endless lines of high doorsteps rising to spacious fan-lighted doorways. Of gleaming brass knockers and polished dark wood. Of houses that were always dusky—even at noon—and always smelled very faintly of the gas from their lights.

Of cousins who looked so much like me in face and dress that I might have been seeing myself in a mirror.

In those days our part of the city was a pleasant clean place—narrow brick-fronted houses, plane trees growing in islands in the cobblestone streets, cool parks where wicker governess carts with their cargo of silent velvet-dressed children rolled through the heavy greenness. Watchmen walked their beats at night, tapping their sticks through the properly empty streets.

The round hollow sound of those nightsticks echoed clearly in my bedroom. The men struck the same places each time, the sounds were repeated exactly, night after night, including a lovely clear metallic ring from far down the block. It must have been the lamppost there.

Our ways too were orderly and proper. My sister and I spent mornings in the schoolroom with our Swiss governess, who taught us German and French and arithmetic. Afternoons we went riding through the parks or set out upon our calls, which in those days were obligatory even for small children. Or so my mother thought.

Almost before I noticed her, my sister disappeared from the

schoolroom. She was sent to St. Mary's to finish her education. Without her, my afternoons became more masculine. I was no longer required to make so many calls. I learned to skate, to play tennis, I even learned to box—it was one of my father's enthusiasms. I was required to spend hours with a fencing master, though I objected violently. I was also taught to shoot with my own small gun.

I saw my parents every evening—if they were in town— just before my bedtime. I had a special quilted velvet robe which I always wore for those occasions. That robe was replaced periodically—as I grew—by others of the same color and pattern.

We were set and methodical and precise in our habits. As, for example, the way we divided our year. Winters were town, summers country. Every year, in the second week of May, we left for the country.

First my father moved to his club; he would follow later, in August, to spend two months with us. My mother saw to the closing of the house; she was a compulsively good house-keeper. My sister arrived home from her school, had her summer wardrobe fitted and sewn, in great rush and confusion. When everything was arranged to my mother's satisfaction, she and her two children, half the household staff, and a large assortment of boxes and trunks all took the train to our farm in Lancaster County.

Occasionally we used our Uncle Robert's private car— which made things much more exciting. It was staffed entirely by Negroes. At first I touched their skins tentatively as if I expected to find beneath them a substance other than flesh and bone. My mother heartily disliked this car, probably because it indicated too clearly that her brother was more successful than her husband. "I would never hurt Robert's feelings," she said, "but this way is just too vulgarly ostentatious."

So it was. Once her opinions were verbalized, my mother never changed her mind.

And my mother's mind had a long reach.

There was, for example, the reason she never set foot in Britain: "I can never forget what they did to Uncle Jonathan." Over a century before, the British shot up Great-Great-Uncle Jonathan's Hudson Valley farm, shot it up so thoroughly that only its thick stone walls kept it standing. It could not possibly have been the American army, my mother explained; they were retreating too rapidly to fire more than an occasional shot over their shoulders. "The British are barbarians," she declared. That those British soldiers were very probably German mercenaries did not influence my mother in the least.

She tried to instill in her children her own very strong moral sense. Every Sunday afternoon my sister and I were called into Mother's parlor, a smallish upstairs room where she entertained her most intimate friends. There we sat side by side on two identical and ornately uncomfortable rosewood chairs while our mother discussed various problems of morality with us. (While my sister was at school, I attended alone.) She must have planned or even written out these mini-sermons—though like any good preacher, she never let us become aware of her notes. She simply walked up and down before us, her long skirts swishing softly, as she lectured us on the good and the proper. I have to this day retained the substance of her lectures—a tribute to the force of her personality. I have always known the Christian thing to do in any given situation. I have simply chosen not to do it.

In any case, thoroughly wrapped, tightly packaged in our web of morals and propriety, we moved through our years and our seasons, from city to country and back again.

Our farm in Lancaster County was prosperous and well run—its dairy herd sleek and beautiful, its barns clean and well painted, its spring rooms stocked with rows of ripening cheeses. The pastures were carefully tended, the hay was the sweetest anywhere. The hothouses and vegetable gardens were legendary. In spring asparagus came to us in the city by special messenger—my parents were devoted to their table and its pleasures. There were orchards too, acres of different apples, green, red, yellow, even some candy-striped ones. And cherries. Every fall the presses ran busily. There was sweet cider, sometimes mixed with cherry juice, and hard cider, apple wine, cherry wine, and—my father's special project— a kind of Calvados, aged carefully in his cellars.

The farm was managed by a tall thin German, a dour man who never smiled, never frowned, and rarely spoke. He had fourteen children by two wives. After six, his first wife died of exhaustion. He promptly married her sister, who proved much hardier. They lived in a large stone house in the midst of the orchards. It was the original farmhouse, I think, its fieldstone walls softened by time and a trickle or two of ivy.

Our road led directly past their front door, but I was not allowed to go there, nor to play with those children. My mother's sense of propriety again.

¶ Our farm was called, with the unintentional arrogance so typical of my family, The Place.

We ourselves lived in the Great House: a huge preten-
tious structure (built by my maternal grandfather), vaguely
Palladio in style, with some Gothic touches. Like the Great
Lantern, which dangled from the mahogany dimness of the
arched ceiling of the entrance hall—a huge tin chandelier,
pagoda-shaped, paneled with colored glass around its sides.
At dusk two men climbed tall ladders to light the half-dozen
small kerosene lanterns within it. Immediately faintly yellow-
ish light sprayed upwards, stalks of light rising like flowers
from a vase. The glass insets threw down little pools of green
and red and blue light, a sifting of strange petals to the rugs
below. Later, as the upper air heated, the lantern moved.
First it shivered, then it swung in slow circles. All the while
solemnly dressed people sat at my parents' long dining table
and ponderously ate their accustomed dinner. Later still,
when the ladies had twittered their way upstairs with a rush
and rustle of skirts, men's laughter shook the dining-room
door and smoke from their cigars hung like banners from
the eaves of the tin pagoda.

I never grew tired, evening after evening, sitting on the
straight carved oak bench my great-grandfather had brought
with him from Wales, next to the suit of armor my father
had brought with him from his student days in Germany—I
never tired of watching the shimmering display of lights in
the gloom.

I've remembered it all these years, and I've seen echoes of
it in the strangest things. . . . In my wife's jewelry . . .
in the shimmering of an Alaskan aurora borealis . . . in the
liquid eye of a Malaysian prostitute.

¶ But I digress. A sign of age. And tedious for everyone. Even me. A mind that will not move precisely and accurately is most unpleasant.

¶ All my summers focused on that lantern with its garish lights and festoons of bluish cigar smoke. In those solitary hours I learned to listen. In the shivering of the dim upper air was a babel of voices and echoes. Yes . . . I experienced something of the future, my future. Not in precise detail, of course. I received no foreknowledge of all the miserable two-legged annoyances who have passed through my bed and my life.

Nothing like that.

But still there were things that the Great Lantern whispered to me in those days when, wrapped in my child's skin and disguised, I watched and studied. And I learned.

Of course I could have learned much more—that was the precisely correct time—had I been left alone to communicate with the dark air. But there were always the rules of propriety. I was always taken from my lantern and put to bed. While, outside my window, the empty nighttime world and the shining groves seemed to be laughing at me.

Even by day my body sang its answer to the beckoning sunlit world. I rode, each morning and each afternoon, with my governess. She was a portly lady who favored large horses and actually looked graceful on them. She had the intense constipated look of all really good riders who are concerned with nothing beyond the movement of the horse and the pleasing tensions of their own muscles. I might have been riding alone.

I saw the entire surface of the earth before me in patterns

of light and shade. Groves where the ground was black at midday. Smooth pastures that ended in an unknown jumble of trees and woods. Places still in the future.

And clearings in the midst of trees—some atavistic memory impelled me to them.

There was one particular place. We never rode that way, there were no paths in that direction. You could see it if you stood at the corner of the croquet green and looked westward. Two slopes of dark trees folded back to show a bit of clearing, a bowl-like amphitheater.

I once asked my governess what grew in that clearing. "Oh nothing," she said after a glance. "It's not a field; a farmer would be out of his mind to bother with anything like that. It's just a clearing. It happens that way sometimes."

That clearing haunted me. I dreamt about it at night. I saw myself riding across the lawn—across the precious manicured croquet lawn—over the fold of the ground and into the open space. Sometimes it was broad day and there were birds singing. And sometimes it was midnight and there was no sound at all, only the moon throwing its moldy light on all sides of me.

¶ So I endured through the days of my childhood. Alone in a tight circle of people, people hired to care for and protect me. Until such time as I should be grown and go my own way. Like my sister.

While I was still a child, my sister became a young lady. On holidays our house buzzed with her friends and her parties. She had begun the long years of breathless social activity that would build inexorably into a triumphantly good marriage. She disappeared from my world.

Oh I still saw her, of course. And with my burgeoning masculine eye, I remarked on her beauty and her charm. But we had ceased to be related.

Do you understand? We had ceased to be related.

I felt like a stranger at her wedding—she eventually married a well-mannered and very rich young man from Chicago. They did nothing at all unusual in their entire lives, except sail on the *Titanic*. And drown.

Then—curiously, very curiously—I felt related to her again. It had taken her death to do it. My sister had returned to the nursery.

But, in those days before my tenth birthday, my sister existed mostly in a series of letters that my mother dutifully read to me. She was visiting friends in Maine, luxurious houses and bleak landscape. She was having the most amusing time in San Francisco; all the men had gone to an illegal prizefight and had gotten into an enormous brawl on a barge in the middle of the Sacramento River. She was eagerly anticipating a proper Continental tour with her aunt and four cousins.

She was gone. Beyond my world. And my interest.

We had always been a loosely connected family. I wonder if even my parents carried any vivid memory of each other. I think they, like all of us, dealt in terms of pictures of each other. Recognized when seen, but not remembered out of sight.

¶ If as a child I often forgot I had a sister, so my parents often forgot they had a son. When my father's glance fell on me—when, say, he looked up from his croquet game (he

was a great player, starkly handsome in his white flannels) —
he would frown slightly, as if he were having trouble identify-
ing me. I look exactly like him, and that perhaps was the
trouble. It must have been like seeing himself through the
wrong end of a telescope.

"Oh yes," he would say finally with great effort, "it's you,
Edward Milton. . . ."

He always used my full name. My mother, on the other
hand, would only call me Edward. "Milton," she said, "is
such a dreadful name. If only your father hadn't read *Paradise
Lost* that year."

I was never aware of my father reading anything at all.
Though I often spent rainy afternoons searching through the
house, I never found his copy of *Paradise Lost*. Ah well, as
good a reason for a name as any other. And I have kept it all
these years. Occasionally my cards have even read E. Milton
Henley. One brash young man—a ticket agent somewhere,
I think—actually called me Miltie. Though he was no more
than half my age, I swung my umbrella, hooked it around his
neck, and gave a sharp tug. He hit his face on the desk in
front of him. After people had stopped being frantic at the
sight of a little blood, I explained to him that I could not
tolerate disrespect to the name of a great poet. His lip was so
swollen he could hardly disagree. (He actually threatened
assault charges, I believe, but my lawyers soon put a stop to
that.)

The thought does amuse me though—my father, during
the long months of my mother's pregnancy, puzzling his way
through *Paradise Lost*. He never mentioned it, so perhaps
he'd forgotten it. Or perhaps he regarded reading it as a kind
of penance, a kind of sympathetic time of troubles to balance

his wife's pregnancy. Yes, I do think it was some kind of un-
conscious impulse of that order. You see, my parents, for all
their casualness, were a very devoted happy couple.

¶ In my tenth year, I did two things: I ended my childhood
and I managed to attract my parents' attention. I got very
sick.

I had never been sick before (hardly a sniffle or a head-
ache) and I have never been sick since. But in my tenth
May I was very close to dying of brain fever.

We were ready to leave for the country, my father had
moved to his club, my mother was completing the last of her
arrangements.

The house was always kept open, you see, but in its summer dress. Woven mats on the floors, slipcovers on the furniture, some light material replacing the winter-dusty velvet
at the windows—and a very much reduced staff, just the
housekeeper and one maid. Even my father's valet moved
with him to the club. But the house remained open. My
parents would have been horrified by any other arrangement.
A man maintained his own home, his own cave, in his own
city. Though he might never set foot inside during the long
summer months, he knew his house waited for its master.

That May, my tenth one, seemed like all the others. Our
trunks were packed and gone. The house was filled with the
usual summer festoons of linen and woven grass. We were
already officially out of town. No one would call on us now.
I, who had been feeling terrible for some weeks, simply
collapsed.

It seemed to me at the time that my head exploded. It had
been aching terribly for days, it throbbed, it pulsed; my fore-

head to my stiff neck was a solid sheet of pain. One morning, on the stair landing, my governess a step behind me, all the pain concentrated in a single spot, expanded, intensified, and my head exploded.

I fainted, there on the carpeted landing, and could not be readily revived.

I can imagine the shrieks and screaming in that house, as my mother suddenly became aware of me.

First she raged at the maids: somehow in taking up the carpets, in packing our summer trunks, they must have disturbed a noxious dust that had sickened me. Then she turned her attention to me. She closed my bedroom windows tightly, hung curtains across them so that no harmful emanations from the street could reach me. The floor was stripped bare and strewn with pine needles, fresh every third day, to dispel the miasma. The pine came from our farm; she had great faith in the healing properties of the woods of her old home.

Nothing worked. I got sicker and sicker. At times it seemed I was floating in the air, at other times I was swimming. But the air was pleasant and the sea was warm, and I did not care. I talked a lot, complete gibberish. "The gift of tongues," my mother said. Nearly eighty years later, I can still hear the awe in her voice. I suppose she was in the midst of one of her religious revivals. She even brought my father to listen: "The gift of tongues!" I don't remember what he said. If he said anything. Or if indeed he remembered who the boy in the bed was.

The doctors (there were any number of them, they always arrived in pairs) told my mother that I was dying. I heard them.

That would be unthinkable now, but before the turn of

the century death was an expected thing. Children died, poor ones and rich ones, and they died of all sorts of different maladies. If death could be predicted in advance, so much the better. There was time to prepare the soul for paradise.

Therefore, because they were responsible men, the doctors told us. I wasn't upset. After all, one of my recurring dreams was of already being dead. From fact to dream and back again didn't seem so horrible. As for my mother, perhaps she shed a few prayerful tears, I don't know. But I do know what else she did. She called all the staff together and had them reopen the summer-stripped double parlors, wax the floors, put down the formal rugs—so the house would be ready for my funeral. My room was over the parlors; I could hear the thumps of moving furniture, and my mother's steady barrage of instructions. It was, oddly enough, rather comforting.

Weeks later, when it was clear that I was going to recover, the whole process was repeated, in the opposite direction. Thumps and thuds and constant commands meant that the funeral formality was coming up and summer mats and slipcovers going down.

What was my illness? Who knows. In those days one was not so interested in the precise names of maladies. A trial sent by God, my mother said. At the time she was obsessed by the idea of purification of the soul through suffering. One of my nurses, a large fat Irish Catholic, a kind and wonderful woman with the open manner of the very stupid, slipped secret holy medals beneath my bed and refused to believe that God had anything to do with my illness. God would never hurt children, she insisted.

Whatever I had, and why ever I had had it, my illness marked the end of my childhood. I had a long and dreary convalescence. My left leg was partially paralyzed—my foot turned in, the weakened muscles would not bear my weight. It was a year before I walked without assistance, a year and a half before I dared try tennis.

I emerged from my cocoon of illness and self-absorption to find that my parents had made plans for me.

❡ Thinking about my funeral had started my parents thinking about my future. And so my education began.

It started with three years in Paris in the house of a distant cousin, Madame Anatol de Boissac, née Amalie Cartright. She was the utterly respectable widow of an unimportant soldier who had died in the Franco-Prussian war. She herself told endless horror stories of the siege of Paris—all unknowing, she had enjoyed deprivation immensely. In her singularly dull life a national catastrophe was, at least, something different.

She, with her housekeeper Mila Lukács and a manservant improbably named Xavier Perot, wore out her declining days in a tall dark house on an insignificant side street not far from the Rue des Réservoirs.

There I walked every afternoon with Mila Lukács. We strolled up and down hoping to catch a glimpse of one of the dozens of dispossessed Slav princelings who sauntered there also.

Mila loved them all, the pouter pigeon ladies whose high-boned lacy collars almost hid their double chins. The little dapper men, looking for all the world like prosperous Parisian bankers. Later I saw those same ridiculous people at the Sunday *corso* in the Bois de Boulogne, driving their phaetons and matched horses as if they mattered to the world.

We did not belong to that international world of unemployed royalty. Amalie de Boissac's relatives (her late husband's family) were without exception prosperous country gentry. We visited them—tedious train rides—on weddings and holy days and family festivals. As my French improved, I began to understand that they disliked each other intensely, but privately. That they resented Amalie Cartright as an American who had stolen their precious Anatol from more deserving French maidens. They also decided that I should marry one of their daughters. It would, so to speak, even things up. Louise was a pretty girl; I kissed her once or twice and I tried to inch my hand up her leg, but each time she ran giggling into the protection of the family circle. Perhaps if she had been more investigative I would have grown to like the entire family. As it was, I loathed them, their broad solid faces radiating self-content and prosperity, their foolish petty interests. They once spent an hour discussing a tannery that a son-in-law had acquired. The very idea of vast amounts of animal skins made my blood chill. Could you, I asked them, preserve human skins the same way and make something useful out of the dead? They found the American child so amusing, someone pressed a small glass of cognac into my hand. . . .

I raged and plotted their destruction. I was rude . . . I slipped a piece of soap into the day's soup . . . I smuggled a stray cat into the milk room and turned it loose . . . I brought rats into the spotlessly clean bedrooms . . . I fought, as they did, in silence and secrecy.

Perhaps my dear old cousin Amalie saw me, or more likely she only suspected me, but she became convinced that she was sheltering a young Dracula under her roof. Quite suddenly I grew tall, girls looked at me on the streets, I began the shadow of a moustache. I had my fifteenth birthday, duly marked by cables from my family at home. The following winter I caught a heavy February cold, and my cousin saw a chance to be rid of me without offending my family. She decided I had tuberculosis, found a doctor who agreed with her, and sent me off to a sanatorium in Switzerland. I was there for only a few months—it was quite obvious that I was not sick at all. My cousin, frantic at the thought of having me back in her house and her life, convinced my parents I should go to a nursing home in Menton. I stayed for almost two years. I loved it all, the sun, the flowers, the comfortable winters. I was so young and healthy that even the constant presence of death failed to upset me. You always knew when a patient's situation worsened. The family, notified by the doctors, immediately began sending flowers and presents. Streams of friends and relatives came to say goodbye. It was as if the doctors had passed sentence of death.

Like Monsieur Janvier. He was a banker from Rouen, a witty man with an enormous supply of scatological jokes. When his flowers began to arrive, he grew uncharacteristically silent. He seemed to be thinking a great deal. He became forgetful; he lost his stories in mid-tale. His wife visited him; after that he refused to talk to anyone. He still walked in the gardens, his shoulders sagging more and more each day. His family sent tempting baskets of special delicacies. He scarcely looked at them. One day he disappeared from the gardens, from his favorite spot under a fragrant fig tree. That morning he had simply not left his bed. The flowers, the presents, the visiting relatives increased. There was a steady procession of messengers to his door. He seemed to be drowning under the onslaught of affection and concern. He sank deeper and deeper under his blankets. His breath grew shallower and shallower until it stopped. He had pulled all the world around him into a tiny circle, like a point of light, and he had then stepped off.

A barbarous world, yes—as barbarous as the de Boissacs and their tanneries and hides. But I no longer noticed. Because the women in Menton were far more available than my foolish little cousin Louise. They did not run away giggling. They said yes, thank you. And please.

Through all of this, my formal education continued. I had a tutor, an honest man, who tried to prepare me for some university. He had very little success, though he himself never admitted failure. His sister Aurélie, who was about thirty, I suppose, became my first mistress. (At least I thought of her as my mistress. Had I been more truthful with myself I would have said that I was one of her many lovers.) She was gay and amusing and naturally lazy and casually sensuous. She skillfully took all my extra money, without once making me feel that I was being cheated. On the contrary. I felt very proud to be contributing to the support of a splendid woman. . . .

I was, as I have said, very young.

I left Menton suntanned and obviously very healthy. My father sent me to London—believing in his muddled way that presence in certain selected places constituted an education. Again I had tutors, but I remember nothing of my studies.

My mother, true to her principles, pretended I was not living in England. Her letters still went to Amalie Cartright de Boissac, who forwarded them to me in London. It all took a very long time of course, but that hardly mattered. My letters to my parents had nothing whatever to do with their letters to me. It was as if we were on parallel tracks, side by side, never crossing.

I disliked England and its military-tinged masculine style. However, its women were delightful and most appreciative of me—quite understandable, with their husbands wasting endless hours in a parody of garrison life. I like to talk to women and I honestly enjoy their company, in bed and out—a response these dear ladies had not met before. It was a powerful aphrodisiac.

I tried to be discreet in my loves, but my wiles were quite infantile. Inevitably, therefore, I found myself in a clammy leather chair in a very proper club talking to Ian Crawford, the senior representative of my family's English connections. (That is how my father's letters always referred to them: connections. How accurate. They were of no interest as people—they were only a way of passing time until my father could be persuaded to let me continue my education on the Continent again.) Mr. Crawford had done extremely well in his business, whatever it was, and he had married a sixth or seventh cousin of the Queen—or was it the King. No matter. She was a dull elderly lady who busied herself with good works for the poor. (Since her husband's business methods had undoubtedly impoverished some of them, it seemed rather the least she could do.) Mr. Crawford stared at the high dark ceiling and said: "I have never had sons, but I will speak to you as a father."

I was so beguiled by that non sequitur I quite lost the next few minutes of his lecture. When I did again listen to the rumbling sound of his voice, I found him warning me against my evil habits. In general terms, of course. But quite definite. There seemed to be a phalanx of husbands ranged against me —a veritable legion. Ready to defend their beds and in them the sanctity of the empire.

Mr. Crawford droned on and on, speaking to the ceiling or

to a distant corner of the room, falling silent when a waiter brought the drink he had signaled for.

As I watched him, I thought: *He is in deep distress. He is speaking his heart and his convictions. And he is funny.*

I was kind enough not to laugh at him. I want full credit for that. I did not laugh.

When he finished—his last peroration was a fervent sigh of relief that duels were no longer in style—he turned to me expectantly. Supposing, I imagine, to find me crushed by the logic of his moral position, reduced to a jelly by fear of all those wrathful husbands.

I folded my hands beneath my chin in what I hoped was a parson-like pose. "Duels," I said, "you mentioned duels. . . ."

"Not done anymore," he assured me hastily. "Not at all."

"One thing has always bothered me," I said seriously. He leaned forward waiting. "A question of propriety. If I should be called out by a husband, and I should kill him. . . ."

He jerked back, surprised.

"If I should happen to kill him, would I then be honor bound to marry the lady in question?"

"I have no idea." His dim wits were beginning to detect mockery. "I do not recall any such incident, though I am fairly well read in history."

"That could be worse than being killed," I said quietly. "Some women are impossible except for an occasional meeting."

He put his hands on his knees and started to rise. "I have offered my advice."

"And I will take your advice," I said sweetly. Half-pleased, half-suspicious, he sat back again.

"I'll leave London before the end of the week." He looked decidedly pleased now. "But let me say a word for myself."

He held up his hand, episcopal-like. "No need, my boy."

"I will tell you in all confidence that I have never once seduced an unmarried woman—no virginities destroyed. Only those husbands you referred to have reason to be concerned."

The puzzled look was returning to his face.

"Concerned. Yes, indeed. They have probably even rushed back to their wives' beds to establish their rights again."

"My dear man . . ."

So I had advanced from dear boy to dear man. Progress.

"Now, when the anticipated and predictable crop of infants arrives, who is to say that my sirelings do not huddle in their nests. Who is to sort my seed from theirs, I wonder."

I left rather hastily after that.

¶ Foolishness. Of course. Utter foolishness. Insult a pompous old fool in the sanctity of his club. Why did I bother? I don't really know. Except that I was still young and not yet indifferent to people. I could still be stung to response, I could still be incited to anger.

I cabled my father for more money, and he, good soul that he was, immediately dispatched it. My bank account was comfortably filled by the time I reached Paris. Feeling dutiful, I paid a call on Amalie de Boissac. "You've grown," she said, and I agreed with her. We had sherry and cookies. She was becoming increasingly fond of her sherry.

¶ (I never saw her again, though I did go to her funeral some four or five years later—I happened to be in Paris at the time. She'd lived to be eighty-one and had spent her last years in a glorious haze of alcohol.

To the great annoyance of her in-laws, those slyly preda-
tory de Boissacs, she left the house to her faithful Mila, the
furnishings to her faithful Xavier, her money equally divided
between them.

It seemed to me a most equitable arrangement. The de
Boissacs talked about going to court to have the will set aside,
but their murmurings subsided quickly. There was nothing
they could do—the will was over thirty years old, Amalie de
Boissac had drawn it up two years after her husband's death,
and it was perfectly correct.

Xavier and Mila promptly announced their pending marriage. Another sensible arrangement. What good was a
house without furniture. Their property and lives must be
decently combined.

I myself helped them through the endless red tape. Mila
did not have French citizenship and Xavier did—that was the
problem. A royal marriage would have been less trouble to
negotiate.

No matter. They were wed, and lived happily ever after.
For a short time at least. Xavier was over seventy, and did not
look healthy to me. I suppose they had a few good years
together and Mila then replaced him. Or perhaps she settled
into the role of dignified widow, like her late employer and
benefactor, Amalie de Boissac.

I never knew what happened to them. I decided that my
part in their life had ended in the marriage registry office.
Even the most amusing situation cannot be prolonged in-
definitely.)

⁋ My education continued. I left Paris for Leipzig. I was now
nineteen, and my father arranged a largely honorary position

with the firm of A. Thadden, ship chandlers. It was a respectable business—my father believed in appearances. It involved no work for me at all, which was the only reason I accepted it. I actually spent most of my time in Berlin.

Though I have not one drop of German blood, I fitted in perfectly with the young Prussians. I spoke their harsh clear language; like theirs my nose was straight at the bridge, flared at the nostrils; my eyes were blue and slightly slanted. I was considerably taller of course (I had finally stopped growing at six-three), but we all affected the same slender wasp-waisted dandyish styles. We drank and fought and flaunted our loves: we behaved like asses in the currently popular manner of fashion. I even considered acquiring a dueling scar (my good friend Ernst Freyhausen had one). I knew that ritual scarification was an ancient and highly respected practice; I knew that scars gave barbaric elegance to commonplace faces like mine. And yet I still decided against it. I don't know what stopped me, so little did in those days. Perhaps I thought such a mark entirely too permanent a commitment to a special way of life. I have never liked permanence.

Still I did envy Ernst his distinguished streak, perfectly placed on his cheek. Though it was almost a year old, it was still liver colored—he worried a great deal about that. He was killed in 1917, and I often wonder whether his scar ever faded to the pale distinction he wanted so very much.

But the Great War was still years in the future. None of us was aware of its approach. We thought only of our own pleasure and of badgering more money from our fathers' pockets. After a year Ernst was posted to Vienna, as military attaché to the embassy. I went home for my sister's wedding. As I've said, she was beautiful; I even began to look at her with less than brotherly eyes. My parents were slower and thicker. There seemed to be a constant sheen of perspiration on my mother's upper lip and on my father's forehead.

I stayed home four months. My father insisted on introducing me to the business.

That phrase—the business—how he loved to roll it on his tongue. It had a particularly holy sound to him; it was an incantation against the spirits of evil.

I was not interested in learning.

My father never once showed anger with me. But soon he fell into the habit of staring vacantly at me during the course of a long morning downtown. To avoid that unpleasant unseeing gaze, I began avoiding his presence. First I stopped riding to work with him. I came late to breakfast; he could not wait for me. I began arriving later and later at the office, while leaving earlier. Faced with two simultaneous defections, he did not know which to attack first. After a few months of this war of attrition, I casually brought up the subject of my returning to Europe. He agreed immediately. He even had something for me in Vienna. My fluent German would be invaluable. I need only spend a week or so learning the basics of munitions manufacture.

That's what it was. My father's father had done very well with a munitions factory during the Civil War (despite being a Quaker), and my father had done quite well with the Indian wars in the West. Now he was interested in a particularly advanced technical process used by the Austrians. I should look into it, he told me; a successful negotiation would benefit both sides.

And so, my introductions in order, off I went to learn something of the business of murder, something of the refinements of the trade of killing.

I have little stomach for the killing of human beings. Why? you ask. I have been a trophy hunter and hold the record for eland and bighorn sheep, and—almost—for elephant. The tiger skins that hang on my hall walls—so dramatic, so beautiful—I myself shot in India. And that is precisely the difference. I kill for trophy or pelt. If I kill a man, I have only an unwieldy object that I must dig a pit for, or dispose of some other way. A waste of my effort.

I am especially appalled by the insane blood lust of civil wars.

The very sort of thing I stumbled into in Belgrade.

I had no business there; I simply wanted to see the city, no more.

I persuaded Ernst Freyhausen to come with me. (At the embassy in Vienna, he seemed to have endless free time and absolutely no duties.) He had not wanted to go, not wanted to leave his new mistress for even a few days. She was a beautiful Hungarian, and he had established her in a hideous apartment, all pink and mirrors.

"My nest," he explained to me in teary camaraderie one evening. He was only maudlin when very drunk. "Why do you want to go to Serbia? Belgrade is a city of pig farmers and the army wears baby booties."

"They wear what?"

"*Opanki,* slip slop, like baby booties."

"Show me when we get there."

"Idiot, don't you know they will have an army coup any day now? Even the *Neue Freie Presse* is predicting it."

He came with me. We were on the last train to enter Serbia before its government closed the frontiers.

That day the Belgrade streets were quiet and orderly, poor mean streets where women dumped dishwater into the gutters. I saw the *opanki* that the soldiers wore—Ernst pointed them out. They were nothing more than handmade shoes, and to my eyes (conditioned by the moccasins of the American frontier) were not at all shocking. There were a few troops milling about uncertainly, half drilling, half lounging, tunics open across hairy stomachs.

Ernst visited his cousin who was military attaché at the Austrian embassy. He returned looking quiet and thoughtful. "They are sure that the coup will be today or tomorrow at the latest. They've offered us the hospitality of the embassy, if you want, until we can get a train. Right now only international trains are going through: no passengers, on or off."

"A secret coup that everybody knows about?"

"The king and the queen don't know. They just sit there in the Konak."

"What the hell is the Konak?"

"Idiot," Ernst said impatiently. "The old Konak is where the king is. You saw it and you don't remember."

We played cards and had supper. In the streets outside there was a great deal of shouting—perhaps it was singing—and a curious generalized low murmuring that seemed to come from nowhere in particular, except perhaps the entire city or the ground beneath it. Later still, near midnight, the street outside my window filled gutter to gutter with marching men, their *opankis* very quiet on the cobbles. The small street light reflected dully from their weapons and their buttons.

Ernst finished the bottle of brandy. "Have these all the time," he assured me. "True Balkan behavior. Makes work for the *kukati*." He fell asleep fully dressed on his bed.

Some troops must have remained loyal to the king; there was a great deal of firing, and finally a series of very loud explosions—all from one direction, though I did not know the city well enough to identify it. I opened the shutters to a red glow in the sky.

I went downstairs. The lobby was completely deserted, the halls empty. I returned to my window.

The glow grew brighter, I could see as clearly as at sunrise. Two men in uniform staggered along drunkenly, arguing loudly. They stopped and with great seriousness urinated together in the middle of the street. A horse and rider went by, not hurrying, just cantering as if on an early morning ride in the park.

Shooting began again, but no longer in one location, as before. These short bursts of fire came from widely scattered directions—some so far away I could scarcely identify them, others very close by. There was no answering fire, no loud explosions. The execution squads were at work. The enemies of the new state were being dispatched by the victors.

A life going out with each scattered burst. Even the sounds of the shots had changed. They were flat and small, solitary and pathetic.

With the early summer light, the city fell silent. Whatever had happened was over.

Later Ernst and I went for a walk. The park-like grounds around the old Konak were filled with people, men and women, soldier and civilian, strolling and chattering calmly, like Viennese on a sunny Sunday. The Konak itself was slightly damaged. Its windows showed jagged glass like broken teeth. Tattered strips of curtain dangled and fluttered from them. A thin feather of blue smoke rose lightly from the roof, delicately tracing across the sky. There was still a fire burning in there somewhere, but no one seemed to notice. Many people had brought or looted food and they were picnicking in small friendly groups. There was even a sort of alfresco banquet at a long cloth-covered table. The dignitaries of the new government, I suppose, were dining. I wondered if those bustling waiters were from the palace staff and if assumption of domestic details was the first duty of a revolution. By the palace wall a small crowd was staring at a tangle of bodies on the ground. Ernst and I hesitated to approach or to ask about them. The whole scene was so insane that we both were shaken and unsure—like being in a madhouse whose rules you don't know. We finally asked two very drunken young officers. First they offered us a drink from their bottles. Then, in very bad French, they informed us that a new king of Serbia would arrive momentarily—he'd been in exile somewhere—and that one of the bodies near the wall was his predecessor on the throne. He and his queen and a few loyal fools had been tossed out the windows during the fighting in the palace.

Their French was too limited to tell us more. They left with protestations of eternal affection—I think that is what they were saying—and wandered off, to find a shady spot to sleep away their revolution.

As we walked back to our hotel I said, "I'd still like to know what happened."

Ernst lifted his eyebrows. "Ask them." And he pointed to a large handsome building across the park.

"Who's that?"

"The Russian embassy. They will have had a hand in this."

He was quite possibly right and I told him so. But what I did not tell him was that the foreign hands could just as easily have belonged to the agents of old Franz Josef. The

Austrian forces, we all had heard, were massed just across the Sava.

No matter. I was not interested in truth telling or the assigning of blame. I was only eager to leave. We managed to get on the evening train.

Of such things was my education composed. Such things go to make a gentleman.

¶ All in all, I was away from the United States for nearly fifteen years. My parents never traveled, but my sister visited me occasionally. Once, I remember, was shortly after her marriage. She and her husband were near the end of a year-long honeymoon, the sort that was fashionable at the time, and they were both weary of traveling and exhausted by the enforced leisure of their happiest year together.

She was also a very diligent correspondent. After struggling through her long spidery handwritten pages, I knew every detail of our family's life. She wrote regularly, on a definite schedule, never unfaithful.

My parents, I suspect, simply forgot about me again. My allowance and my extra incidental expenses were handled automatically by my father's office staff. My steady progression through a series of impressive business titles and affiliations seemed more like a previously arranged battle plan than any demonstration of parental concern. Even my father's letters, which were invariably dated ten days apart, sounded so completely and totally unlike him that I suspect he merely delegated somebody in the office to "write a letter to my son." My mother wrote much less frequently. Her letters tended to be an odd assortment of newspaper clippings:

articles and bits of news that she found interesting. That was, I suppose, easier for her than trying to think of something to say to a son she couldn't remember.

(Perhaps I am just easy to forget. I myself have had periods of difficulty remembering who I am. Not the facts, of course. I could always recite my name and current address. But there have been times when I did not feel like my name. Times when it took an effort of will to wrap my identity around me, to put flesh on the bones, skin on the skull.)

Typically then, when my father died my mother forgot to notify me. Some days after his funeral, my sister discovered the omission. She immediately sent cables to Paris and to Vienna, to be sure of reaching me. I was in neither place. I was in Marienbad, watching the wealthy and powerful and famous of Mittel-Europa saunter pompously about, sipping at their tiny glasses of foul-tasting wonder-working water.

When I returned to Vienna, I found her cable in the accumulation of bills and letters and invitations. I was more surprised than shocked. I had always thought of my father as eternal, when I thought of him at all.

Of course I answered her immediately, explaining my silence. I do not think my message had left the telegraph office in Vienna before a second cable arrived, this one announcing our mother's death. She had survived her husband by only three weeks.

"Even in death they were not separated," my sister wired dramatically.

Each would, I imagine, have been lost without the other, such is the force of habit.

I went home then, I did not need my sister's subsequent

frantic urgings. I knew what I must do. I knew too that I would not be coming back to Europe. I had had my play time. Now it was over.

¶ I took my father's place. I did rapidly what he had never been able to persuade me to do—I learned the business. I was competent and skillful, as I always knew I could be. I led the busy life of a successful businessman and eligible bachelor. I played tennis and croquet, went on picnics and houseparties, flirted mildly, and avoided serious entanglements.

I even spent some dreary days at my sister's summer place on Boston's north shore. I loathed it. The huge ugly houses (my sister told me proudly that some of them had a hundred rooms), the pervasive chill in their walls (none of them was winterized or adequately heated)—I always managed to leave a few days early. Each time my sister seemed more amused than hurt by my hasty departure. She herself fitted into the scene splendidly.

Now of course the pressure was on me to marry; and even I was susceptible to it. I met my first wife one rainy afternoon at the Palmer House in Chicago, when I gallantly gave them (her mother was with her) my own taxi. Her name was Abigail Morton, she was visiting in Chicago, she lived in Sacramento, California, and her father was "in cattle." While her mother and I played the usual game of mutual friends (we found them fairly rapidly; the Mortons were cousins of my brother-in-law's stepsister in San Francisco), I watched Abigail carefully. She was indeed very pretty, a small blue-eyed blonde with a lightly turned-up nose and a slightly pouting mouth that hinted of temper and other delights. Some months later, my sister invited them to stay with her in Chicago, adding coyly that I too would be there.

We became engaged. Back Abigail went—across the endless continent on that dirty exhausting train—to have her trousseau made in California. Ridiculous ritual, this mating dance. After a decent interval I too took the train west, accompanied by my sister and her husband. It was all a great bore.

My wedding was the last time I set foot in the state of California.

¶ There were a great many things wrong with our marriage. That pouting little mouth did indeed indicate temper, and a very quick one; the bright blue eyes covered a brain that was really quite incapable of learning anything new. She was as impenetrable as a fossil. And much less interesting. Also, her father was a great annoyance. He was always badgering me for a loan. After a very few years of marriage I found myself an unwilling partner in a failing Western cattle empire.

Still, Abigail and I stayed married, held together no doubt by mutual boredom. The one serious and finally fatal disagreement we had was over my son.

¶ As I've said before, my sister and her husband were among that glittering group on board the *Titanic*. She wrote me from London before sailing, her usual chatty long letter. I was then in Denver, negotiating for the purchase of some mining properties. I had become quite interested in the future of the old silver mines.

The news was in huge black headlines in every paper, every word sharp and final in that clear dry air of Colorado, and I thought: *So that is the end of my beautiful, gentle sister.*

There were no names listed at first, but I had no hope.

I felt that she was dead; I took the train to New York immediately. And waited there.

His body was eventually recovered. Hers was not.

¶ My wife, Abigail, arrived to comfort me. I sent her back home, not even allowing her time to unpack a single bag.

I could not stand the sight of her beautiful blue eyes knowing that my sister was dead.

I kept to my hotel in a state of near-panic.

A selfish feeling, I am sure. (I am always selfish.)

The hand of God had struck too close to me. I could smell the chilly ozone of eternity.

I decided to strike back. I would father a child. The conventional thing to do, of course. Matter of fact, I was delighted to find I was so basically conventional—it is always a pleasure to discover something unknown and unsuspected in oneself.

But I digress.

My mind made up, my plans definite and settled, I emerged from my hotel, summoned my wife to New York. Together, dressed in mourning black, we escorted my brother-in-law's body back to Chicago, where his family waited. We buried him there with all the pomp and ceremony he would

have wanted. Next to him we raised a memorial to my
sister, as of course she would have wanted.

And all this time my plans became clearer and clearer. I
knew that my child must, so to speak, burst from the brow of
Jove, or rise like Venus from the sea foam. It must be mine
alone, it must have no blood attachment to any of my wives
—by then I could predict, quite accurately, a series of them.

Within two months of my sister's death, I found the perfect incubator for my child. A young Irish girl, of no importance whatever. She met all my requirements: she was
quite young, sixteen, intelligent, a virgin. She was very well
paid for her trouble, which can't have been all that onerous
to a young healthy woman. She seemed delighted with the
whole arrangement. As well she might be. The money I
paid her—it was a lump sum of ten thousand dollars, a great
deal in those days of 1912—was quite enough to fetch
her a decent husband, a thing she could never have aspired
to before. In nine months she leaped from penniless immi-
grant domestic to middle-class respectable woman.

My only requirement was that she disappear completely.
And so she did. I bought her a ticket to San Francisco, with
the understanding that she was free to leave the train at any
stop west of Pittsburgh.

We parted with the proper pleasantries, like two partners
in a concluded business deal.

The child was a boy. He was strong and lively, as I had expected from the mating of two healthy young people. I
named him Stephen, a name that has never been used in my
family. I wanted him to be unique in everything.

I intended to adopt him at once. But my wife Abigail
would not hear of it; she possessed the firm resolve of all
very stupid people.

I first told her of my plans shortly after I made my initial decision. I don't think she believed me. She was extremely conventional herself and could not understand that others might be different.

When I announced the child's arrival, Abigail had one of her famous temper tantrums. I ignored her.

She went back to her parents in Sacramento. I knew they would send her back to me. And they did.

While she was gone, in the marvelous quiet of the house, I brought home my son. He looked a great deal like me, except that his eyes seemed to be dark blue, but this, I knew, was usual with newborns.

The nursery was functioning happily and efficiently when my wife returned.

She banged through the front door, quite knocking aside the butler. (She must have forgotten her keys, or perhaps she merely wanted to make an entrance.) She stamped into my study, where I sat reading. Her chin jutted out like a boxer's, and her superb eyes actually seemed to shoot blue crystals of light.

"I am home," she announced.

"Yes." I went back to my book. "I thought I heard you."

We made up. We still had a life to live together. And, if I may say so, with all my wives I have tried very hard to be adaptable and kind.

Abigail persisted in her foolish impossible behavior. She would not give up the idea that if anybody had borne my child, it should have been she. To hear her talk, one would have thought it was her absolute right.

I grew quite weary of her dynastic importunities and her father's financial ones. Finally I refused all credit to that endless appetite in California. I had had enough. My patience with Abigail wore thin also. Stephen of course continued to live with me as my son despite his clouded legal status.

Abigail and I drifted into divorce, a tedious and costly solution in those days. She (at her family's urging) demanded an astronomical settlement. I was reduced to using faked evidence of her nonexistent infidelities—how sordid. But then I had little choice in the matter. I did give her a handsome support settlement, and, as I expected, she soon married again, and I was free of her at last.

¶ My second wife, Eleanor Halsey, was delighted with my plan to adopt Stephen. (All my wives are most docile in the first three years of marriage; after that they become stubborn and opinionated.) During our short courtship, she practically begged me to begin adoption proceedings. I did so the second day after our wedding.

My son Stephen reached his rightful place, and I was content.

Eleanor was genuinely fond of him: her maternal instincts were strong. She soon thought of him as her own child, and he was most certainly the only child she would ever have from me. Eleanor was a sensible woman—I was much fonder of her than any of my other wives, and our marriage lasted longer.

¶ My son Stephen was quiet and totally self-contained. He was wary; he considered things long and carefully. Even as a very small child he had what I can only describe as a judicial air. Perhaps it was the result of his early years with Abigail.

Though she was never abusive toward him, she was scarcely cordial either. He could not fail to be affected by that.

I myself tried hard to amuse him. One year—he was five or so—he was infatuated with ponies. I bought him a cart and four beautifully matched roans, extraordinary animals. Stephen considered them gravely, said thank you properly and without any warmth. To this day I don't know if he really liked them.

And the monkeys. Oh yes, the monkeys. For his eighth birthday, we (Eleanor and I) built a large greenhouse as a tropical jungle for two pet monkeys. We re-created quite successfully the natural conditions of Brazil, and the monkeys thrived. We added a flock of brilliant birds; they too did well. Stephen spent every free moment there, in that special exotic world. But playing so carefully, so gravely. As if he were afraid of breaking a single flower or bruising a single leaf.

Eleanor and Stephen seemed happy together. He often did his schoolwork seated next to her. You could hear them giggling their way through his lessons. By the third grade he was correcting her mistakes in arithmetic, by the fourth or fifth he was improving her prose style. They both found that very amusing. At thirteen he left for prep school and Eleanor grieved openly. She constantly found flimsy excuses to visit him.

¶ My friends congratulated me on Stephen—the perfect son, they often called him. I myself was never so sure. I was beginning to suspect that the scatter-shot fallout of the genetic code had defeated me. There was something in him . . . how can I say this? At times he seemed so predictable, so open and clear, like the sand bottom of a shallow lake. Then, abruptly, he changed completely, vanished.

The Stephen phenomenon. It reminds me of something I read once in a book on astronomy. In our nicely organized skies, charted for millions of light-years in all directions, there are mysterious empty spots, black holes, they're called. Areas telescopes do not penetrate. Closed and unknown.

Within my son there were such areas, obscured and baffling to me.

Still, in many ways Stephen was indeed the perfect son. He was polite, respectful, diligent, handsome. He was an excellent student, and his teachers admired him. In prep school he refused to take part in athletics. "I cannot agree with the concept of an all-around man," he wrote me. "If I have only so much physical energy, I do not choose to dissipate it racing around a frozen muddy field." His school, impressed by the fact that he was the first serious Greek scholar they had had in a hundred years, agreed with him.

He wrote long letters to me, serious well-reasoned discussions of subjects that interested him. There were no personal details at all.

A lifelong habit, his letter writing. I kept them all, neatly filed away. Occasionally, every five years or so, I would compare the latest with the very first, the letters of a prep-school boy with the letters of a mature man. They were remarkably alike. Of course the man's expression was smoother, the vocabulary larger, the references more apt—but both were secretive and impersonal. They might have been written to anybody. There was nothing filial about them.

Stephen finished prep school and went on to Princeton, explaining himself by letter, as usual. "I should perhaps have gone to Harvard," he wrote. "There is certainly no greater scholar-teacher than Professor Wolfson. But I do not think that I, at this stage of my intellectual development, am sufficiently prepared to be his student."

Typical of Stephen to explain what he did in terms of what he did not do.

At Princeton Stephen's academic record was impeccable—he seemed interested in absolutely nothing beyond his books. I teased him about that once. He refused to answer. A few days later, as I expected, I received a letter defending his position. The first line was "You must understand, Father, that the pursuit of knowledge is my love."

And so, I suppose, it was.

He made it perfectly clear that he could never join me in business. (And perhaps that was lucky; I am as much a loner, in my way, as is Stephen.) With his passion for the classical languages, his quiet studious ways, I assumed that he would settle into a dusty Chair at some university. I was not prepared for the letter that announced, in his last year of college, that he was entering the Unitarian ministry.

I took the very next train to Princeton, my arguments ready. I was not objecting to the ministry—as a matter of fact I am devoted to fancy Episcopalian services. Choirs and vestments and incense, echoes of an opulent past. Moral ritual totally divorced from daily life.

But not this.

At the Junction I hired a taxi and drove to the college. Stephen was not expecting me. I'd been so annoyed I'd forgotten to telephone. I had no idea of his class schedule; so, after checking his room, I simply wandered about more or less aimlessly. Some two hours later I found him walking briskly toward the library. He was actually whistling cheerfully.

I myself was irritated and angered by the delay. And I said so.

"Father, if you'd just told me, I would have met you anywhere at any time."

There is nothing more infuriating than a dutiful answer. And furthermore, beyond my son's handsome façade I saw clearer than ever that gleaming impenetrable self. . . .

"Dear God, Stephen," I said more emphatically than I had intended, "I had no idea that you were considering the church. Absolutely no idea. Now, there is no need to tell me that you are quite able to manage your own life. . . . If you have decided on the church, why then the church it will be. . . . But, if you must hear the call, why don't you hear it from a respectable church? Does it have to be Unitarian?"

Stephen smiled and said nothing. Only a slight clouding of his eyes told me that I had offended him.

I had not meant to. But would he know that?

¶ My son persevered in his choice and eventually was called to a church in Shelby, Pennsylvania. I visited him there, was polite to everybody, and pretended not to notice the dank dirtiness of the town.

I telephoned Stephen regularly. And he wrote his usual long letters, though his typewriter was so bad I could scarcely read them. Finally I sent him a new machine and a note saying, "This is not a present, it is a form of self-defense." He sent me a copy of his first publication, a translation of Juvenal. It was a rather nice-looking book by Boni and Liveright, I believe. He had dedicated it to me and I thanked him quite properly.

We were in contact but scarcely in communication. Our

relations were now those of two grown men of widely diverging interests.

He wrote to announce his impending marriage—the only short letter I have ever had from him. (Incidentally, though I'd spoken to him a few days before, he'd said nothing about it.)

"On Wednesday, June 21"—it was now the nineteenth—"I marry Lucy Roundtree Evans. We shall be returning directly home to Shelby, and we shall both be writing you soon."

That was all, the entire letter. I telephoned his house immediately: no answer. He had gone to fetch home his bride.

Obviously he had not wanted me to attend his wedding. Neither did I want to. But I do think he might have given me the choice.

Within the week, as he had promised, I had a letter from my daughter-in-law.

"I am sure you must be wondering what sort of woman your son has married. May I describe myself?" (What idiocy.) "I am twenty-eight" (he had married an old woman), "a native of British East Africa." (My grandchildren will be black, dear God!) "My father is Edwin Roundtree, born in London, my mother is Anna Vorster, born in Pretoria." (The image of mixed-blood children faded. The lady was obviously a mixture of English and Boer; she would have a round head and faded coloring.) "My first husband, Harold Evans, died some years ago, we had no children. I have been teaching at Greenwood College, but now all my time will be devoted to my husband and my home."

The letter went on and on. It read like an answer to a job advertisement.

And yet, when I am being fair, which I rarely am, I realize

that in her place I myself would have used exactly the same direct approach.

Very soon they came to call on me. Stephen had actually taken time from his precious flock to present his wife to his father.

Lucy Roundtree Evans Henley was, as I had guessed, homely. She was too tall, every bit as tall as Stephen. She was far too thin. Not the sort of thinness that comes of illness, but the gaunt transparent look that comes from too little food. She had no-color brown hair and light brown eyes. She wore no makeup beyond a dusting of pale powder on her small hooked nose. She still had a trace of the British colonial accent, but it was not unpleasant. As a matter of fact, her voice was the best thing about her, soft, but resonant and very clear, and completely without the fashionable female singsong.

To be truthful, had I met her first, I most certainly would have tried to seduce her. And she most certainly would have refused me. As it was, I disliked her immediately and intensely.

I determined to be disagreeable. I refused to offer them so much as a drink of water. They ignored me. Stephen rang for the maid (whom he had known since childhood) and ordered tea. He even took Lucy into the kitchen to meet the cook, another old friend of his. When tea came, I pretended not to see it. So Lucy poured, uninvited. (Quite gracefully, I must admit.) I declined everything, though the almond cookies on the tray were among my favorites.

"Father," Stephen said, "Lucy has written children's books."

"I rarely read them anymore."

She laughed, that impossible woman laughed. And Stephen

with her. They drank their tea and ate the almond cookies and told me all about their plans for their foolish church, for their hideous little house, for their entire lives.

The sobbing end of shabby gentility.

I sat and listened. What else could I do? He was my son.

The afternoon wore on. When they paused for breath, I asked Lucy, "Are you pregnant?"

Stephen said: "That is a rude question, Father."

"Not really," Lucy said. "It is only a frank question." She turned to me. "No, I did not marry your son because I was pregnant. On the other hand, there is no reason why I cannot bear children. My first marriage was childless by choice."

Damn the woman's smug reasonableness.

"Since you ask" (now she was reminding me that I myself had introduced the subject!), "Stephen and I plan to have two children as soon as possible. We are neither of us very young, and if we want a family we must begin at once."

"Two children? What a wretched number."

"Well, Father . . ." She saw me wince at the word and stopped immediately. "Shall I call you Mr. Henley?"

Again, what could I do? English is such a limited language. For lack of any alternative word, she must call me Father. . . .

"We will have two children because we know we can afford two children."

So it was simply a matter of money. . . . After they'd gone, I called my office to look up my son's income, the bits and pieces of things he'd been given on birthdays and Christmases in his childhood. It did not amount to very much. The salary from his church would be even less.

They must have a wedding present then. I had my lawyers transfer a block of ten thousand shares of Delaware Electric to my son. It would pay well enough to add comfort and more children to his household.

My gift was returned. The only message was an unsigned note in Stephen's handwriting: "Thank you, Father, but no."

¶ But again that was the future. Long before Stephen had even finished college, Eleanor and I reached the parting of our ways.

I can't exactly claim Eleanor as a mistake of my youth, I was thirty-five when we married. She had probably the worst taste of anyone I'd ever known—that spoiled our marriage as much as anything else. Her parents had died when she was in her mid-teens, leaving her not only quite wealthy but also the possessor of some of the most atrociously vulgar jewelry created by man. She wore it constantly, in a garish jumble.

As I have already said, one evening when she was dressed for the opera, I told her, "My dear, you remind me of a chandelier at my parents' country place. All those colored stones like flashing lights."

I meant it rather kindly, the memory of that chandelier *was* dear to me. She was not impressed.

Quite frankly, the bejeweled winking twinkling mountains of her flesh appalled me. She had always been plump—or so I seem to remember. At the end of a marriage it is difficult to recall the beginning. With the passing years, oh, how she grew, how she puffed, how she threatened to fill the world with her self. Her elaborate jewelry, eternal tribute to her family's barbaric taste, rested on flesh as soft as lard and very nearly the same color. The only piece I'd ever given her, an extraordinary cat's-eye pendant, she often wore—poor soul, no doubt she thought to please me. But alas, against her skin the stone lost its terrible animal gleam. It lay horizontally on her breasts, offered to me, the good husband, for all the world like a strange egg on a plate.

It was her arms that most disturbed me, those perfect rounds of skin, so soft, so delicate that even bracelets bruised them.

As a relief from Eleanor, I found Guido O'Connor. Of course his name wasn't Guido, it was probably something like James or Shaun, but he would never tell me. He was twenty, dark-haired and green-eyed. He was short and slight, very hard and very angular. His arms were ropy with strands of muscle, his legs distorted with sinew. He was exactly what I needed after years of drowning in Eleanor.

Guido moved into the house as my valet, and Eleanor moved out in a rage. He was with me for less than a year, a foolish time for me. Men are not my taste at all, I've had only three or four in my whole long life, and Guido certainly was the worst. He knew nothing about the care of clothes and did not choose to learn. Eventually I tired of badly pressed suits, muddy shoes. Even those muscular arms, hairless as a woman's, no longer moved me so greatly. Guido left.

I saw him only once more, some four or five years later. He was having trouble finding a job and he needed money. Since it was then the middle of the Depression, I thought he was quite probably telling the truth. I gave him the money—he was surly and insulting about taking it, but of course he did. One needs to eat.

I have no idea what happened to him. And I sometimes wonder why I gave him that money. Had he been a woman I would most certainly have not.

My third wife I find hard to remember. She was German, her name was Lenore and we agreed to go our own ways amicably after six months of marriage. Sara, my fourth wife, was a beautiful dark-haired girl from Mobile, Alabama. During our brief marriage she hardly left the house. She spent all her time reading novels in her bedroom, alone. One day she walked out, leaving the front door open. And disappeared. I notified all the proper authorities and hired my own detectives to search for her. They discovered absolutely nothing. She was eventually declared legally dead, I believe. But by then I had long since gone my own way.

Shortly after Sara vanished, I found a new and overwhelming interest. As usual, with a woman. I became a publisher of multicolor art books, while supporting an expensive and ambitious quarterly called *The Arts*. Its title sprawled across the cover in a tricky Gothic script that nobody could read. It was a very serious magazine, full of high purpose, like its editor, Helen Reed. We were together four or five years—I actually took an apartment in New York, actually moved there. Helen, though she kept her own apartment, spent most of her time with me. She was a handsome woman, a little too tall, a little too thin, with thick gray hair pulled into a bun. A schoolteacher's face, a pedant's seriousness.

I did not marry Helen. With age one becomes more wary, more eager to avoid trouble. After four attempts I simply stopped going through the farce of a marriage ceremony.

My affection for Helen faded, as, alas, my loves always seem to do. I really think she exhausted me into indifference. She herself had to live at a high pitch of intellectual excitement; she was the most breathless woman I have ever known, as she bounded from interest to interest, all of them overwhelming. Inevitably the increasing difference in our attitudes led to quarrels.

She left in furious tears one afternoon. She crammed all her belongings (how had she accumulated so many things here?) into three large suitcases, two of them mine. (Since they were Vuitton, I did not expect her to return them; she did not.) I offered her the car and driver; she refused silently by turning her back on me. I concluded that I had done all a rational man could. I fixed myself a Scotch and kicked life into the living-room fire.

Half an hour later, crossing the room for my second drink, I happened to glance out the window into the rather miserable street. There she was at the curb with her suitcases, waiting for a cab, pacing up and down impatiently.

I began work on my carving. It was a wooden figure, two feet high, an Indian in full ceremonial dress. I had started it simply to annoy Helen. Now it was very nearly finished, except for the elaborate headgear. I was doing each feather with absolute precision. I had no trouble with rachis and vane; the fluff was very difficult indeed. After nearly an hour, my hand was tired.

Helen was no longer at the curb. I opened the window and looked down the street. There she was; she had not gone more than a few hundred feet. She was dragging a suitcase in each hand, unable to lift them from the pavement, and kicking a third along in front of her. She heard the window open, spun about, glared at me, just as the paper boy came around the corner. He'd finished his route and was going home, with him the very large wagon he used for his deliveries. Thanks to him Helen found a way to exit with dignity, stalking behind a rattling wagon piled with suitcases.

Some weeks later I heard from her lawyer. She was threatening to sue for breach of promise, based on certain of my letters, he said. I simply hung up on him. I write very nearly the same letter to every woman. They are invitations to adultery, not promises of marriage.

I saw Helen again twenty years later. Someone introduced us then, I would not have recognized the hunched old woman. Perhaps she felt the same about me. . . .

¶ My son Stephen is very fond of a quotation from Ecclesiastes concerning the alternations of opposites: war and peace, love and hate, life and death. He seems to take comfort in this instability. I may indeed have my seasons but I do not enjoy them. When I love, I don't want to think that very soon I shall be hating. I want to think that each love is eternal, that we shall live happily together ever after. Even when I know perfectly well that we shall not.

I prefer to see my life as a pageant. Or a processional. Like that wonderful march in *Aïda* in which once, as a boy, I was a costume extra. I paraded across the stage, raced around back, exchanged my spear for a banner. Then across the stage again. At one point I even drove in a chariot, my armor hidden under a hastily wrapped toga, on my head a garland of paper leaves.

Now in my old age things look more unreal to me than those costumed figures in *Aïda*. A trick of the observer's eye, no doubt, a senile astigmatism.

I am no longer active in business; I devote myself to philanthropy. It is, in its way, as amusing as making money. I built a school for my son's congregation; with their financing problems I didn't think they would ever have one otherwise. My son was very nervous about it; he didn't approve, but he couldn't think of a reasonable objection. (I find it hard to believe that thin gray old man *is* my son.) I added a small wing to the children's hospital there (my son was equally nervous about that; I don't think he cares to have me in what he regards as his territory). I am presently deciding the best way to endow a few neighborhood baby clinics.

All of it for children. Yes, I realize that. I am fond of youth. That is probably why, after almost six years, I still keep Roberta. She is thirty now, which to me is a veritable infant. Her skin still has the glow of young tissue. She is quite beautiful and worth every penny she costs me.

And she is very expensive—her clothes, her apartment, her allowance. I even sent her younger sister to college, then to the Sorbonne for two years. Is there indeed a younger sister? I have my doubts. But I am amused by Roberta, and her flaming beauty—she is a true redhead—fits perfectly into my processional view of life.

My son was appalled by her. "A simple adventuress." He actually used that old-fashioned phrase. My son, as you see, is a very limited man. As I suppose a minister must be.

Roberta was, for some years, my live-out mistress. I often introduced her that way: it made her simply furious. She claimed it hurt her pride. Now, the very idea of Roberta with pride is indescribably hilarious to me.

Two years ago the role of my live-out mistress abruptly changed. I was unable to prevent it at the time.

I had a coronary. One morning at my desk I had the most absurd feeling of not being able to breathe. I thought of heart —at my age one does—but there was no pain, no pain at all. Quite automatically I rang for my secretary. Equally automatically I put my pen back in its holder. And then I stopped breathing completely.

Or so it seemed. When next I remember, I was ensnared in

a tangle of wires and hissing valves and surrounded by busy white-coated people. And oh yes, Roberta was there, her frightening hair pulled back into a bun, her face as free of makeup as any nun's.

Months later when I left the hospital, I found that she had moved into my house. For my sake, as she put it, she had sublet her apartment, furnished of course, and had crammed all her most personal belongings into half the upstairs closets of my house. She had also taken over the bedroom next to mine, after doing a little work on it first—rug and bed were white fur, blue damask walls and curtains. Just a place where she could rest, she assured me, from the strenuous anxiety of caring for me.

She was, as a matter of fact, a very good housekeeper. She got on well with the three shifts of nurses, though they were all utter harridans. She charmed my fretful suspicious cook, soothed the feelings of the butler. And sought out ways to be gently amusing and totally delightful to me. It was in many ways her best performance.

(I sometimes think that Roberta, like me, sees her life as a series of pageants. This was her Domestic Idyll.)

I recovered, though it was almost six months before I felt like moving about freely. I discharged those white-capped witches who had so completely controlled me. Then I set about returning Roberta to her proper place.

One Wednesday she went shopping, promising to be gone all afternoon. She was, of course, meeting a man; I applauded silently: her true shopping expeditions left me only a mountain of bills. This way was far better.

While she was gone, I mobilized the house staff, very much the way my mother had done for my funeral so long ago. We, helped by the two strong Polish dailies, gathered all Roberta's things, packed them into large brown boxes, carried them down the front stairs, through the house, past the pantry, through the kitchen (this is an old-fashioned house), and into the small wing behind the second summer kitchen. It was originally the servants' wing, but since I do not keep that sort of staff anymore, the four small rooms were empty and waiting. The two dailies chose the very first room—the boxes were heavy and awkward, and they were tired of the carrying. (The butler, the cook, and I, being almost equally dotty and ancient, were of very little help.) We hung some clothes in the closets, but most we left in the boxes. It was just too difficult to unpack completely. I myself brought the flowers from her other room—a big sprig of purple California lilac. I knew she was very fond of it. I simply removed it from its blue vase (eighteenth-century Japanese, very valuable; it had been on a shelf in the downstairs library before she had appropriated it) and put it in a more suitable container. In this case a Mason jar.

She threatened to leave, of course. Filled with the curious elation that follows a coronary, I ignored the scenes. And she stayed. Of course, I know that she is looking for another spot, that she will eventually go. I shall miss her. She was so very decorative.

But I shall not miss her as much as I once might have. I think perhaps I have tired of women and their ways. At last. And I have grown very fond of my great-grandchildren. (My son's two children have each produced two children: I am haunted by that number.) They are as curious about me as I about them—and I always censor the story of my life for their hearing.

STEPHEN
HENLEY

¶ Yes. My father. If only a bit of his physical stamina had been passed on to me. It wasn't, as you see. In my sixtieth year I have asthma, emphysema, and diabetes. My skin wraps an assortment of ill-functioning systems. I hear myself whirr and sputter like a badly tuned engine. . . . I am also becoming forgetful. Not seriously so. Not yet. But even this small loss of memory worries me. I suppose I shall eventually begin to forget who I am and where I live. I shall eventually become one of those old men who sit on park benches, open fly and empty mind, whom young patrolmen, with an elaborate mocking show of courtesy, drive home. Yes, I'm sure that's what I shall be. Pathetic. Pitiful. An embarrassment.

Not at all like my father. Pity is not an emotion my father inspires. Anger and hate, these are what he produces in people. He is the sort of man who ought to live in violence— only he doesn't. I don't think anyone has ever raised a hand to him in anger. He's only experienced a sort of silent violence, the violence of intent, of feeling, not of action. I doubt that he himself was even aware of it.

If I asked, he would say that he did not plan for violence, that it had no place in his scheme of things. I'm sure he'd say that. Because more than anything else, my father is convinced that he alone manages his life.

And I suppose he does. Even his aging body, which is so rapidly collapsing into the dissolution of the grave, still obeys him. Each morning, at his direction, obedient creaking muscles heave fragile thinning bones over the bed's edge. When he says think, his hemorrhage-speckled brain obediently clicks its remaining synapses. I've noticed no impairment in his mental powers—though he says he has noticed a deterioration in mine. And he is probably right.

That's another thing about my father, his observations are most often quite accurate.

My father's great strength has always been his ability to see things singly and to act on them singly. Ignoring everything else. I myself never have been able to do that. Not even the simplest event, not even a single happening in time and space. I have to see all around it, to embellish it. I meet a soldier named Harold and I see Hastings Field—despite the fact that Harold is a corporal in the 101st Airborne. A woman named Ruth, and I see the stooped shape gleaning in the barley field at Bethlehem. . . . I have confused and tangled myself in so many lines of logic and thought and history.

At prep school, when other boys decorated their walls with large photos of horses, or properly severe family groups, including dogs, or discreetly gowned young ladies (always identified as their sisters; the authorities allowed no other young female images), my walls held only two framed mottoes. One was "Know Thyself." At the time I thought it possible. The other was "It is a terrible thing to fall into the hands of a Living God." When I woke at night, in the dim light I could see only the last words, "Living God." How strange for me, who do not believe in any kind of god. . . .

But I was speaking of violence. My father has cultivated hate and lived serenely, unmarred by any action. I, of gentle respectable habits, found myself in violent action. It happened like this.

One cold wet spring morning, as I repaired the sermon announcement box on the lawn of my church, three men ran down the street. I saw them only as blurred shapes: my distance glasses were still in my shirt pocket. I smiled and bowed to them anyway—they might be my neighbors out for a morning jog.

I went home early for lunch. The kitchen window was open; smells of lamb and onions floated out like ribbons. Scotch broth. We had it for lunch every second Tuesday, following every second Sunday's leg of lamb. I could construct a calendar in terms of my wife's menus, they are so reliable. As we always do, my wife Lucy and I sat down to a cup of coffee. She began describing at great length a new voter-education program; she was far too absorbed to notice the arrival of a blue-and-white police car.

Now, the last time the police came because a parishioner had killed his wife and they wanted me to break the news gently to their children. . . . I ran quickly through our present membership, found none I thought capable of violence, and breathed a little easier as I stood up.

"What?" my wife said, interrupting herself.

"The door."

"It hasn't rung."

"It will." That was the sort of joke we enjoyed, my wife and I. We were a gentle elderly couple.

I knew the policeman by sight; his name was Ted. He was excited, and talking very fast. His voice fuzzed indistinctly in my hearing aid.

"Please speak more slowly," I said. "It's hard for me to understand otherwise."

My wife, whose hearing is perfect, was sitting with her mouth slightly open. She was struck dumb—as my father would say, quite an accomplishment.

Ted announced with laborious slowness: "There's been a holdup. Vince Costello sent me to get you. If you'll come."

What could I say? Vince Costello was the police chief, a perfectly sensible man. We served together on the town Parks and Playgrounds Commission.

Ted and I raced across town with the pulsing wail of a siren and came finally to a squealing stop.

I knew all this from television—police cars parked at odd angles; men crouched behind them.

Vince Costello was waiting. He was a small slight man, nervous and balding. During long meetings of the Parks and Playgrounds Commission, he munched Gelusil tablets and poked, wincing, at his stomach with one finger.

"Mr. Henley," he said.

"Good afternoon." As if we were passing on a corner.

A small flat pop and a rattle of glass—out of sight but quite close by.

"Every now and then he shoots a window out," Vince Costello said.

For a moment I was tempted not to believe him. In movies guns had a larger, more dangerous sound.

"Well"—Vince Costello hitched up his pants—"this was just your usual liquor store holdup, maybe we'd pick them up later, maybe we wouldn't. Either way, no sweat. Except that they had a brand-new car, stole it in Richmond Park yesterday. They jump in, put it in reverse, hit the gas, and try to make a sharp turn. . . . You can guess what happened."

"No," I said.

"Mr. Henley"—Vince Costello tapped his ulcer and grimaced—"a new car with the latest pollution devices, you handle it like that and it is going to do just exactly one thing. It's going to stall. Only by this time the manager's hit the burglar alarm and he's got out his own gun. So they took off running, and after a few blocks, they saw the school. And that is where they are. With the second and third grades and two nun teachers."

I remembered: three men, running. Not joggers after all. My hazy vision had not noticed their guns. I'd nodded and smiled at them. Politely.

"Now they want you, I guess." Vince rubbed his stomach again. "They say they want to talk to the minister from the Unitarian church, no name. But they say they'll recognize you."

How suspiciously he looked at me. As if we hadn't spent hours in tedious debate over the placement of sandboxes and swings. . . .

I looked down at my dirty brown pants, my torn yellow sweater. They were the clothes I had worn this morning. Perhaps the men would recognize me. "I hope they don't shoot before they see who I am."

"We'll tell them." Within a half-minute I heard booming amplified voices announce my coming.

Like a nineteenth-century gentleman ascending the great stairs to dinner.

"What am I supposed to say?"

"How the hell would I know," Vince said testily.

"I will do the best I can, then."

"You do that."

The school was built above the street on a low terrace. It was originally a grassy rise, but children's feet had worn it into troughs and cracks and furrows. The few green blotches on its sides looked more like mold than grass. Nothing moved; nobody looked out the windows as I climbed the steps.

When I was three or four feet away, the door swung out-
ward. A man with a shotgun stood there. He was a Negro,
quite dark, with a slight Afro. "Come in, Reverend," he said.
"Sorry about jumping out at you like that, but I got to be
careful."

"It's all right," I said.

"Yeah? It was Snake's idea, sending for you." He was still
staring at me, trying to gauge my capacity for negotiation.
"Room 6."

The other two men were there with the children and the
nuns. The stench was nauseating.

"Why don't you open the windows?"

"We ain't opening anything," one of the men answered.

"Snake don't smell," said the man who had met me at the
door.

So that was Snake, who'd wanted to send for me. A short
heavy man, with the long sad face of a Mexican Indian, the
bedraggled air of the last of the Mayas.

"Windows aren't any protection," I told him patiently.
"The police can shoot through them. If you can't smell,
you're all right, but what about the rest of us?"

He blinked at me a couple of times and I thought how I
had seen him in the Orozco murals in Mexico City. Then he
began opening the windows. "Shitty kids," he said.

And there it was, under the desks in the center of the
room: two small piles of feces, soft and runny. The children
were terrified. There were pools of urine too. I was standing
in one. I stepped out of it.

"They won't let us pray or sing," one of the nuns said.

"Maybe they don't like music," I said thoughtfully, not
really meaning it that way.

Snake began to cackle. The third man, whose name I

never knew, moved to the open window. "Keep the kids from shitting all over," he ordered. "Next one does it, eats it."

"They're afraid," one nun said hesitantly.

"Oh, be quiet." I sat on the edge of the teacher's desk. "We've got enough trouble."

The man who had met me at the door sat on the other side of the desk. We were side by side, just his gun crosswise on the desk between us. "Preacher's right," he said. And then, abruptly: "Call me Rock."

"My name is Henley," I said, accepting the introduction.

"I know," he said. "Saw it on your sign."

"You did?" I said, staring into his bloodshot black eyes. They were puffy like exploding raisins.

He smiled at me and his teeth were lined with gold. "Snake over there, he can see anything for miles around, saw your sign as we run past."

"Can't smell," Snake said, "but sure as hell can see."

"Well," I said, "well, yes."

He might have been a ship's lookout, up the mast, out on the prow: Land Ho. Yonder cloud marks land: Greenland, Helleland. . . . He'd have a name: Olaf the Eagle Eye. Edmund the Scout. . . .

But he was only a scruffy man trying to escape the police. And all the strength of his eye muscles had been used only to read my name.

Rock jabbed me with his gun. It was friendly enough, he used the butt end.

"You falling asleep on me?"

"I was trying to think what to do next."

"You don't have to think. You just carry messages. In. Out."

And that is exactly what I did. Back and forth, six times,

ten times. A state police helicopter circled low overhead. Rock fired at it through the open window.

"You hit it?"

"With a shotgun?"

"You were shooting at it."

"Jesus," he said wearily, "you don't know nothing."

"Keep the helicopter away," I told the police. "It makes them nervous."

"We noticed," Vince Costello said. "What are they asking now?"

Mostly they wanted a car. Sometimes they wanted a plane and sometimes they seemed to forget about that. The Snake wanted them to get his wife. She refused to come. When the police got too insistent, she screamed so loudly that neighbors came running. I didn't tell Snake that. I told him that they were having trouble locating her, that she seemed to be out shopping. He grunted and looked at me over that shriveled useless nose. Maybe he knew her pretty well.

If they hadn't been so slow, if they hadn't dragged out the negotiations so endlessly—I think the town police would have given them a car. If they'd just settled quickly.

But they didn't. And soon there was a small army of police and state troopers. There were even a few men in plainclothes who were supposed to be FBI, and who stood aside and watched, as detached as sparrows on a telephone line.

And finally the governor. He was elected on a safe-streets platform just last year—the sort of honest man who believes his own slogans. So his orders were definite and clear: No deals, no arrangements, no planes, no cars.

"I am not going to tell them that," I said.

"You think they'll kill?"

I hitched myself up on the fender of the patrol car. "The guns are loaded," I said. It was impossible to explain to him. That reeking room. Children whimpering under their breaths. Nuns' rosaries rattling like bones. You could smell fear too; it oozed through Rock's skin, it was on his breath when he leaned close to talk to me: a bit like acetone on a diabetic's breath. Of course Snake couldn't smell it. Maybe that was why he seemed the calmest.

"Don't ask me questions I can't answer. I'm too tired to think."

It wasn't ever going to end. We'd all be here until we died and our skeletons held our positions. . . . I would still be running back and forth. Achieving nothing on either side.

"Okay," Vince Costello said, "just take it easy." He must have been in the habit of shaving every afternoon; stubble showed black and heavy across his cheeks and lip. He rubbed at it constantly, as if it itched.

"Mr. Costello, we have sat in too many Parks and Playgrounds meetings. You and I know most about the placement of swings and sandboxes. . . ."

I blew an imaginary smoke ring in the air and wished I could have a cigarette. I had had to stop with the first sign of my emphysema.

Muffled orders, dragging clanking sounds. They were maneuvering lights into some sort of planned position. If they *were* lights. . . . What if they were some fantastic new weapon, programmed to distinguish the bad guys from the good. . . . But Buck Rogers was dead. And when the shooting started there'd be no difference, criminal or victim. Somebody would get killed. What great funerals, what incense, what singing. If the children were young enough, they might even have those lovely Masses of the Angels, all gold and white. Joy in death. Freedom of angels. Sacrifice and triumph.

There. My mind simply would not behave. I must have some food.

Costello said, "Tell them the governor will talk to them on the phone."

So back I went. Up to the corner, turn left, right at the steps. Inside the door, Rock was waiting.

"You got something new, Reverend?"

The phone rang. He jumped and I jumped and I thought he was going to shoot me. Then he stepped between me and the phone, lifted his gun, and fired. He had calculated his angle carefully, the pellets scattered off along the hall. Away from us. The phone stopped ringing.

"That was the governor," I said.

"We aren't talking anymore."

In the classroom two or three girls had fallen asleep, huddled against the wall. Fear does that sometimes to young children.

"You're not doing so good, Reverend," Rock said.

I sat in the teacher's chair. I seemed to be finding more and more excuses to sit down. "I've gone up and down that street a dozen times. Every time I walk out of here I wonder if the police are going to shoot. And when I come back I wonder about you. You need a soldier, not a minister."

"Okay, okay," Rock said. "What about the car and the plane?"

"The governor said to tell you that you won't be harmed and you will be treated fairly. I guess that's what he was going to say on the telephone."

Rock's face grew thinner. He needs a burnoose, I thought,

and a camel and big desert spaces behind him, and an old-fashioned rifle with silver workings all over the stock. Like a Berber.

"They are fixing to kill us," he said softly. His narrowed face quivered as the news ran along its muscles.

"Look," I said, "you come out and talk to them. I'll come with you."

The shimmering eyes stared at me. And slowly, calculatingly, he nodded. "Okay. But if anything goes wrong, you get killed."

I relaxed. I had got him to agree to something. "I'm an old man." I smiled my most beatific clerical smile. "I have for all practical purposes lived my life. I'm not likely to be frightened by threats now."

He muttered something. His face quivered and narrowed again. *Good lord*, I thought, *he'll end like a playing card figure.*

Snake and the other man said, in a single breath: "Yeah." Like a sigh.

"Okay," Rock said. "Let's go."

I nodded, stood up, began to walk toward the door. Rock said to one of the nuns: "Come on."

She stood speechless, staring. Snake swung his gun slightly and shot out another window. The glass crumbled away down the slope outside.

"Let her stay here," I said.

"Shut up," Rock said.

"She's likely to faint; you've scared her out of her wits. If she stumbles or falls, nothing's going to stop the police shooting."

"Huuuuuu," Snake whistled.

Rock thought. Then: "You go first. Tell them I'm coming.

I'll take a kid." He reached for the nearest one—an ordinary-looking boy, he might have played Tom Sawyer.

When I stepped outside I could sense the muzzles of all the different guns point at me.

I walked methodically, counting so that I would not hurry. Firmly, evenly. I saw two police cars parked crosswise at the corner. They hadn't been there before.

Close by, crouched behind a house, Vince Costello called softly: "Get under cover." He motioned me to join him.

And all at once I was very tired of people telling me what to do, I was tired of running errands, I was tired of substituting for a telephone. I had had enough.

"What are you doing there?" I said, standing perfectly still. "Why did you come so close?"

He motioned again, more violently.

"Did you ever think how silly you look, cowering down like that?"

"Will you get under cover, for God's sake!" he hissed angrily.

"But I don't believe in God. . . ." I was really very light-headed. My blood sugar, of course. I hadn't eaten on schedule. There were so many things wrong with me.

A man with a small camera was taking pictures over Costello's shoulder.

"One of them is coming out now, with a child," I said. "To talk to you directly."

Something moved in Costello's eyes. Fear? Uncertainty? *But, my dear, I wouldn't know what to say to His Highness.*

"His name is Rock." I spoke very slowly, as if to a child or a foreigner. "He's the dominant one." Just to be sure, I translated. "I mean, the others will do what he tells them."

And then a kind of a hiss, a whistle, a ripple of sound. I turned. Rock and the boy had come outside and were standing at the top of the terrace. He had his gun in one hand and the boy's shoulder in the other.

In all their secret places the police shifted and caught their breath.

I walked slowly back toward the school, not knowing what I wanted to do.

Behind me Costello said softly, "Damn old fool." And in a different voice: "It's yours, Turnbull."

I knew Turnbull. He'd been a schoolteacher once, then a coach, and then a policeman. His hobby was target shooting. I often saw his picture in the local paper next to a trophy he'd won.

Rock and the boy were not coming down the steps. They moved across the grassy stretch at the top of the terrace, following the wall of the building, the boy on the outside.

And then I saw. From here, with the boy, there was no clear shot. But if a man were far to my left, there was going to come a moment when a small clear angle appeared.

I opened my mouth and no sound came out. Rock was looking steadily at me. Maybe because I had carried so many messages back and forth, he expected me to have one now.

Turnbull fired, Rock spun into the building wall, the boy tumbled down the slope toward me. I grabbed him, uncertain whether to put him in front of me or behind—I hadn't the slightest idea where the shots had come from.

Later they asked me to say a few final words over Rock's body. "I'm not a Catholic priest," I said. "You'll want a priest for that." So they got the fire department chaplain, in his white slicker, to pray over the hunched pile of clothes.

That was after Snake and the third man had surrendered, shivering with fear, pants stained with urine.

¶ Vince Costello said to me: "You didn't have to tell me what dominant meant."

How sensitive people were. Maybe he really did belong with me on the Parks and Playgrounds Commission.

¶ The news pictures were dramatic and totally misleading. I was in the center, holding the boy, you could see the tips of the police guns and you could see Rock plastered against the wall, held there by bullets like nails.

And oh yes, my father. He telephoned immediately. "How do you get into these preposterous situations. No matter. You were brave, courageous, heroic. You were very very impressive. . . ." He chuckled loudly as he hung up.

The next day he sent a huge silver bowl filled with pears and figs. The refreshment of ancient warriors. The symbols of manhood. . . . My father's knowledge has always amazed me.

So for about a week, my wife and I, in our breakfast room behind gingham curtains, munched away on the strength of ancient warriors.

"Well," my wife said, when the fruit was finally gone, eaten or spoiled, "I'll put the bowl in the dining room."

Because there were just two of us, we rarely used that room. The bowl sat undisturbed in the middle of our small maple table. Occasionally, while she dusted, my wife put it in the open window; in the light it winked like an evil eye across the narrow driveway.

It was rather lovely in its way—vaguely Monteith in style,

Italian silver, with lion heads and rings on each end. My father's jokes were often expensive.

Like his car. That year he had a pale green Cadillac limousine. He had it repainted several times to get the precisely right color to set off Roberta's flaming hair. (My wife said the car reminded her of nothing so much as a green pea pod with two rare peas inside.)

All his life my father was a collector of beautiful women. Living with him, I too developed a trained and knowledgeable eye. Unlike him, I am quite impartial. I admire beauty in women, but I am not moved to possess them in any way. Sex has always seemed to me a waste of energy, too time-consuming and too complicated—more than a bit like the game of Go.

Roberta was the most flamboyant woman my father had ever had. Her hair was an incredible red, somewhere between carrot and auburn. Her skin was white and flawless. Her eyes were wide, black-lashed, and a true violet.

Actually she was not more beautiful than many of the others. She was just more highly colored. My father had not used to like this type. It was as if in his ancient age his sight had dimmed, and his perceptions weakened. And he needed more brilliant plumage to stimulate his fading senses.

One afternoon the green limousine slid silently to the curb outside. Roberta rang the bell. The chauffeur helped my father up the steps. He came through the door, regally. "You are looking well, my dear," he said to Lucy, and then to me: "None but the brave deserves the fair."

Dryden provided him with quotations for all occasions.

"Father, this is hardly a world of heroes and cowards," said Lucy.

"Ah yes." He settled down in the big chair. Roberta adjusted the stool for his gouty left foot. "You subscribe to the doctrine of necessities . . . such nonsense. Why be ashamed of the word brave? Where's the bowl?"

Lucy put it on the coffee table.

"Dwarfs the entire room. Why don't you get a bigger house?"

"We expect to be retiring next year."

"Retiring from what?"

"The ministry."

He snorted. "Impossible." He pointed to his bowl. "What do you propose to do with this?"

"I don't know," I said honestly.

"It looks a bit like a baby's bath," my wife said peevishly. (I made a mental note to tease her about that later: she prides herself on her forbearance.)

My father was delighted. "You are absolutely right. Roberta, turn it around, I want to see . . . by God, it *is* a baby bath." He leaned back and grinned beatifically. "We have discovered a perfectly good ecclesiastical vessel. You can baptize babies. . . . Marvelous, baptize babies. Better than the porphyry the old Dagos had. Much cleaner. If the monsters pee in it, sterilize it. Think of that, Roberta, getting rid of original sin in an eleven-thousand-dollar silver bowl!"

"I do not baptize, Father," I said patiently. "You know that. And I do not believe in original sin."

"Ah," my father said, "don't you feel the weight of it sometimes?"

"I do not."

"Clouds of glory then?"

"Not that either."

My father said, "I myself enjoy feeling guilty."

(Of course he didn't. My father did not feel guilt or re-
morse. His deepest emotion was amusement—he had in a
sense lived a life with one theme, comedy.)

Waving Roberta away, he began to discuss the financing
of his pediatric clinics. When he was serious his blue eyes
turned slate color. . . . His endowment plans were careful,
generous, and about as secure as any human could make
them. We were clearly going to have an excellent community
pediatric service for a long time to come.

"Father," I said, "some of this money could be put into
geriatric services too."

"Absolutely not."

"Always children?"

"I am a dirty old man."

That was not a satisfactory answer, but then my father
was never in the habit of being satisfying. I turned to listen
to Roberta and my wife. They were discussing Japanese
calligraphy, and Roberta was saying: "I lived in Tokyo until
I was fifteen."

Roberta in Japan. Imagine. My father's women were always interesting. One of them (during my school years) was
a fifty-year-old Middle European. Rumanian, I think. She
represented such a change in my father's taste that even he
felt called upon to explain. "Alma," he said, "has been the
mistress of very nearly every great man in Europe. Her appeal
is totally catholic. Politicians, architects, musicians . . ."

"And you, Father, what are you looking for?"

"Their footsteps, Stephen."

Seeing the disgust on my face, he added, "You have the
soul of a priest. A good priest," he corrected.

Alma was a charming lady, not at all the great whore of

Babylon I'd expected. I just never managed to see her clearly. She was obscured by her past loves. All those famous names seemed to wrap around her like fog, blurring her outlines.

She once offered me the use of her bed, as a gesture of friendliness. I declined. She seemed so overwhelmingly competent that I was terrified. If I ventured into her depths, I thought, I would certainly drown.

The women my father brought to me were too beautiful, too accomplished, too polished. I did not wish to be mated with an accomplished courtesan. (How my father laughed when I described my feelings!)

But my father did not win. The choice of woman was mine. Her name was Constance Smither and she was seventeen. As was I. She went to St. Agnes, I went to Hutchinson, both schools in Weston Fells, Maine. There were so many prep schools in that small town that the whole place had acquired a kind of outsized junior look—its symphony, its opera, its theater were all staffed by teenagers. (Long before baroque music was popular, you heard its thin pure line rolling across the grubby snow-streaked yards of Weston Fells.) Its main street had four ice cream shops, all shining marble and glittering chrome spigots; half a dozen clothing stores filled with student styles; and four florists—those were the days of large dances and ribbon-tied corsages.

The town's adults existed on the edge of our lilliputian world, all their needs gathered under one faded sign: "Dry Goods Store."

There was an optometrist—so many of the students were nearsighted—with the latest in New York frames. (We all seemed to turn to New York in those days, sunflowers bending toward the sun.) There were two dentists, one of whom was also the town abortionist. At the age of eighty he finally retired—his shaking hands no longer able to deal safely with the delicate young bodies of the girls—to live with his daughter in Los Angeles. The town bade him an emotional goodbye. (Though out of school by then, I still read the local paper.) There was a parade. There was a picnic at Tremaine Park, by the little can-littered river whose water was absolutely yellow with filth. And after dark, there was a great fireworks display. He was a nice man, Doctor Phillips. I went to him several times to have my cavities repaired.

The town also had a physician named Larsen, who was an alcoholic with a hip flask for office hours. He treated colds and flu and an occasional coronary, and diphtheria and mumps and measles. He also treated venereal diseases quietly and discreetly with no word to parent or school.

For me those were years when lights glittered and air quivered and the foolish naked stems of jonquils were unbearably beautiful. It was the glory of the old revival hymns. Nothing more nor less than glory.

But—Constance Smither. I loved her for the hidden light that always seemed to shimmer softly on her yellow hair. In the Youth Symphony she played second violin and I played cello, so I was able to stare directly across the arc and study her. In the tedious hours of rehearsal, I memorized her, inch by inch, starting with the crown of her head—a fuzz of hair there, new shoots not yet trained by her brush—to her feet —she wore the stockings and black oxfords of St. Agnes School. One spring evening, during the Third Beethoven, in the long boredom of the last minutes, I thought, clear as billboard print: *Her. I will have her.* We droned into the dreary thumps of the coda. My mind sparkled with the brilliant emptiness of a winter night, I shivered in my icy clarity. And I made my plans. The orchestra was going to New

York for a regional competition. My father lived only a few hours away. . . .

After rehearsal, as always, we drank hot chocolate in a narrow stuffy hall called the cloakroom. I elbowed my way to Constance. "I've been meaning to ask you," I said with a casual air, "when we play in New York, would you like to skip out one evening and have dinner with my father?"

She had small fine teeth that looked abnormally sharp, a bit like the ones savages file into points. She showed them now, in her proper smile. "Do you think St. Agnes will allow it?"

"My father will be in touch with them," I said.

And so he was.

From Mrs. Abbott, my father's housekeeper, I got a box of his stationery, his old-fashioned heavy Tiffany paper. I wrote the letter myself, by hand; a typewriter seemed somewhat out of character. The housekeeper intercepted the answer— not difficult at all. Neither my father nor Eleanor (to whom he was still married at the time) would be home for weeks.

I called for Constance with my father's car and driver. (I even remembered to have that man wear his proper black suit: at the time my father affected a chauffeur in gold knickers and fancy Russian shirts—that would not do for me.) During the long drive, I held her hand very gently. We swept through the entrance, the car immediately disappeared toward the garages, I opened the front door into a brightly lit but empty house.

Constance giggled, sending a shiver down my spine. "Stephen, let's explore; imagine having a whole house to ourselves."

So we raced up and down stairs, opening doors, peering in closets.

"Is your father married?"

I tried to sound sophisticatedly casual. "Sometimes," I said.
"What a strange family you have."
"Not really."
"Yes really."
I kissed her on the lips, directly, firmly. They were too soft,
her lips, and they were cool. The effect was vaguely familiar
and vaguely unpleasant.

She blushed. She had a heart-shaped face, high cheek-
bones, and small chin, and she blushed so deeply that she
looked like a Valentine heart. I found that more exciting
than the feel of her lips.

"Your hair looks much better loose." I flipped out the pins
and the comb that held it up in a formal sweep.

"Aren't we going to have anything to eat?" she said with
that little giggle of hers.

Our supper was waiting for us in the small downstairs
study, the one with paneled walls and comfortable English
furniture. The fire was burning softly, the small table was set
with blue china and a lace cloth, and a low bowl of spring
flowers.

(Mrs. Abbott had outdone herself. I should owe her my
allowance for the next month without any doubt.)

"Do you always have supper like this?"

"Only with special people," I said. And held her chair
with my best imitation of Douglas Fairbanks.

There was chicken and sturgeon and brilliant pink salmon
and oysters decorated with caviar on a bed of ice.

After a few glasses of champagne Constance allowed me
to open the buttons of her dress. That was all, she said. Ever
so gradually the dress eased itself off her shoulders and
dropped to her elbows, so that she sat there naked from the
waist up, drinking champagne, while I sat on the other side

of the small round table, fully dressed, twirling my glass. It was unbelievably glorious and exciting.

With a great flourish I filled my glass and went to stand by the fire.

"Why are you doing that?" she asked.

"Because the warmth feels good."

"I will too." She stumbled over her sagging dress. "Oh dear."

"Slip out of it and come toast yourself at the fire." Douglas Fairbanks would have been proud of that line.

With a sigh she bent toward the fire, naked breasts turning red in the glow. She was more plump than I had thought. She had round full breasts and oval buttocks and wide white hips.

"The Lord will punish us," she said very softly.

"Of course he won't."

I stepped behind her, slipped my arms under hers and put my hands over her two breasts. She straightened up at once and stood quietly. "Come along," I said.

We raced through the hall, up the stairs, to my bedroom. In the soft cool linen of my bed I discovered that I was still dressed. While she watched silently, her blue eyes enormous in her small face, I fumbled aud cursed at my clothes. My coat dropped to the rug, tie crumpled beside it. I ripped open my shirt. My fingers, so skillful with her dress, no longer worked properly. There was a high-pitched hissing in my head, a steady rhythmic throbbing. My bones ached as if they were broken. I did not see clearly. The whole world ran to me and gathered in me. I grew and grew and filled the universe. Until there was nothing beyond me. Nothing, nothing at all. Just empty space.

Never again in my life did I feel desire like that. Not ever again.

Not even with Constance. We met some seven or eight times. Kindly exploring ventures, gently satisfying to both of us. But for me the desire was gone.

It was as if I'd been born and died at once. That my first woman had been my last.

Do I make myself clear? There was no more desire. There was mechanics, there was duty, and finally there was relief when my wife and I, tired of each other's bodies, slipped from all activity.

Do I make myself clear? The end was a joy. When I finally realized it *was* the end, I felt—how shall I say this?— an echoing surge, a shadow of a dimly remembered burst of joy and power. Exactly the same, but smaller, dimmer, a ghost of a shadow of the beginning.

I seemed to have been looking for the end. I reached it with a far faint echo of happiness.

¶ I did not marry until I was twenty-six; my wife was two years older. My entire congregation was much relieved— they found something very suspect about a single man. They had been urging me, not at all subtly, to find a wife, and they rejoiced with me when I did.

I first met Lucy while I was still at Princeton. She was married to Harold Evans, another student. I saw her only twice, very briefly. She seemed to have no part in campus life. I did however know her husband fairly well. We were both members of a discussion group that met every Saturday afternoon. He was a slight wiry man with a Rupert Brooke look, flowing ties and soft poetic collars. There was about him an air of concentrated energy, of danger and far places. He had been adventuring among archaeological ruins in Turkey, I think it was, had been declared persona non grata by the government, and expelled. He had reportedly smuggled out any number of early Greek artifacts and a few very valuable Mycenaean pots. He was also a brilliant archaeological scholar. Furthermore, he was a cryptographer working on the Minoan Linear B script. People at Princeton said his work—though incomplete—was very much like the later successful attempts of Michael Ventris. Without any doubt, Harold Evans was at the beginning of a very fine career. Until one morning a university janitor found him in the chemistry amphitheater. He had blown himself apart with a shotgun. A most effective way out of this life, but then I guess he knew exactly what he was doing.

Well, whatever. . . . Mrs. Harold Evans closed their apartment and left for Barnard College (I lost sight of her at this point) and eventually took a job teaching Latin and Spanish and French at Greenwood College, Virginia. I finished Princeton and went on to the ministry.

Some years later, in 1937, I met Lucy Evans again. Quite by accident. (No wonder the Greeks deified chance as Tyche; she plays such an important part in all our lives.)

I was attending a Unitarian Conference in Greenwood, Virginia, a favorite place for such gatherings. Lucy Evans came to one of our evening meetings.

I recognized her at once. I do not think she remembered me, though she politely insisted that she did. No matter. I called on her the very next afternoon. We walked the winding brick paths of the college, admiring the brilliant rhododendrons and the spectacular views of the valley below.

I, who am not given to impulse judgments, found myself instantly certain: I would marry Lucy Roundtree Evans.

She was intelligent and serious and well read. She had a scholar's respect for learning. She was gentle and patient with her students, though their finishing school chatter must have been very trying to her.

These were the obvious reasons. But they did not explain the immediate sympathy I felt toward her, the sense of familiarity, of having known her for a very long time.

There were other simpler things. . . . Her height. When we stood and talked, her eyes were on a level with mine. When we walked, her stride matched mine. . . . Surreptitiously I monitored the pattern of her breathing and found that it echoed mine perfectly. . . . She was not beautiful in a fashionable way. Her skin flushed too easily from wind and sun, her shoulders were too square and thin. But she walked—how can I say this?—as if she belonged on the earth. Her heels left imprints on every surface, testimony to her passing.

We courted, if that is the word, almost entirely by letter. Roads were bad in those days; train connections, through Philadelphia and Washington, were slow. I was unable to leave my church very often, and the rules of propriety prevented Lucy from visiting me. I suppose, in the two years we corresponded, I traveled to Greenwood only a dozen times. No matter. Letters sufficed. We were both of an age to consider marriage calmly and without undue passion, to assess the degree of contentment we would find together. Also, though we never spoke of this, I knew that Lucy needed to free herself of the memory of Harold Evans.

We were married June 21, 1939, in the college chapel. Lucy's mother, who had been visiting in London, came to the ceremony. I did not invite my father. I would have found his presence too disruptive. As a matter of fact, until just before our marriage, I had told him nothing about Lucy, not even the bare fact of her existence. I rather imagine that he had long ago in his own mind assigned me the role of crusty old bachelor.

Lucy and I visited him soon after our marriage, of course. He was obviously annoyed and quite rude. Lucy managed nicely. And I do think that before we left, he had come to have a kind of grudging regard for her.

I asked her opinion of him.

"He's your father," she said.

No more, no less.

A few months later my father telephoned me. "Your wife needs more security than you can give her," he said, and there was no trace of mockery in his voice. "Especially if she produces those two children you have planned."

"My salary is adequate, Father. I can only tell you that over and over again. Please don't send us any more presents."

"What I propose is a kind of life insurance," he said crisply. "If you live, I do nothing. If you die, I establish a trust fund for your wife, to be used at her discretion. Are we agreed?"

A thoughtful gesture, confirming my opinion that he had indeed been impressed by Lucy's character.

"Explain our arrangement to your wife," he said, still brusque and businesslike. "Tell her the trust will be an outright gift, so that she need never deal with me. I know she will find that a pleasant prospect."

¶ A year after our marriage Lucy bore a son, Thomas. The following year we had a second son, Paul. Both are married now with children of their own. Both have done well. Thomas is a microbiologist at Indiana University. Paul is with an investment counseling firm in Chicago.

Thirty-four years of marriage, and I can describe it in a single sentence: We met, we married decently, we bred, we are now about the business of growing old and dying.

Just so.

I would have much more to say about my work. All in all, I am fairly well pleased with what I have done. I think I have increased dramatically the interest in liberal religion in my town. No other Unitarian church has shown such continuous growth. Also, our cultural program is quite innovative.

(I began that program in 1943, during a period of acute personal misery. I'd joined the army immediately after Pearl Harbor—I was not yet thirty, in good health, and the services needed young chaplains. Eight months later I was home with a medical discharge. I'd spent all but a single week of my military career in the hospital—both my legs were broken when a jeep skidded and flipped over on me. I knew that I was lucky—the other passenger and the driver were killed—but for months after my release I was plagued not only by physical pain but by a sense of worthlessness, of futility. To mitigate my depression, Lucy suggested I organize a cultural program for the church. She thought the congregation would welcome it. She was absolutely right. My ideas found an immediate and enthusiastic reception. Over the years the program has expanded steadily.)

Our Great Books Series on Monday evenings never has less than a hundred people. Our theater group introduced the plays of Brecht to this part of the country years ago. Each spring we manage to produce one of the chamber operas, and quite creditably at that. And our regular Thursday Recorder Consort draws people from miles around. Our community service programs do well, too. Our voter drives have been a great success, as has our campaign for fair and open government. And lately, we have devoted ourselves to organizing a program of drug-control centers.

These projects now—each has its touches of humor, each its annoyances—I could talk endlessly about them. But not my family. About them there is nothing to say.

¶ Now I am retiring to Florida. My wife Lucy is enthusiastic. She is so glad to be rid of the long damp winters, she says, and the endless gray skies.

I was never aware that the weather affected her so. I thought her more intellectual, more able to make herself into a perfectly isolated point, a self-contained whole, without demands or needs.

I myself rarely notice places. Today at breakfast, Lucy asked me the color of our house. We have lived here all our married years, and the color has never been changed, she says. I guessed tan. It is actually a dark green stain.

I am not totally unobservant, however. I notice the progression of the seasons in the small garden outside my study window, green to brown to white of frost and snow. I wait for the tulips that grow there every spring, and for the white rhododendron, and the small clumps of midsummer daisies.

I notice beauty. But I am not interested in the shelter that keeps the rain from my head.

I shall be perfectly content in Florida, but I am in no hurry to leave here. Lucy, however, waits with ill-conceived impatience. A sixty-two-year-old woman as restless as a child.

Were the rattling palm fronds so beguiling? What sirens were singing this song to her? What instinct drove her to this appointed place? To this elephant graveyard where we would end our days, where we would deposit our bones in the sandy soil. . . .

I felt a sudden flood of feeling for her, not lust, not love. Something deeper, something older, something asexually human. The sympathy of blood for blood, of aching chalky bone for aching chalky bone, of skin for familiar skin, of brain for familiar creased companion. The visceral sympathy of acquired identity.

There was one thing I could do. I went to my bank box and looked through the jewelry my stepmother Eleanor Halsey had left me. As I sorted through the jumble of stone and metal, her ghost floated beside me. She was the mother I recalled, soft and easy with flesh. When I hugged her, I rested on undulating oceans. She loved jewelry, wore far too much of it. My father complained loudly, especially when she combined the superb cat's-eye he had given her with a pair of dangling moonstone earrings of supposedly Russian origin.

Their arguments echo from fifty years ago.

"Those earrings are the best reason I know for shooting the Czar."

"I like them."

"They are spoiling my cat's-eye."

He was right, of course. She had no taste, poor lady, but if I ever think of a mother, I think of her.

When she died, some fifteen years ago, her jewelry went to me, her money went to a Methodist hospital in Missouri. She remembered my father with a single nasty comment: "For the most miserable years of my life," and she returned to him his own collection of pornographic art that she had somehow contrived to spirit away in the heat of the divorce. It was really an amazing collection, the pornographic side of great artists. I remember a Watteau, a Fragonard, a Picasso; I've forgotten the others.

"Well," said my father when the crated canvases, discreetly wrapped, were delivered to him. "How nice of her to return my property." He looked, considered, and put the whole collection in storage. "They all seem to resemble Eleanor."

I found the cat's-eye, held it up, tried to imagine Lucy wearing it. . . . No. Too near her own coloring. For her it would be almost like wearing an artificial eye on a chain. . . . I finally selected a set of antique garnets, necklace, earrings, brooch. I had seen similar ones in portraits of the late eighteenth century.

I had the pieces cleaned and polished, lest they have what my father found in his pictures: a mist of Eleanor lingering about them.

When I gave them to Lucy, she immediately went out and bought a very expensive dress to wear with them. I had never known her to do that before.

¶ My father was here yesterday, with his two lawyers, to complete the last details of the pediatric clinics. We met with the city manager, an unpleasant sort of man, irrationally suspicious. Like all his type, he simply cannot believe that people give money away. But he is very greedy, and if by any miraculous chance something is given away, he wants to be sure he has a share in the credit.

I found the meeting tiring. My father, for all his advanced

age and debility, found it amusing and exhilarating. Especially the city manager. "A self-made son of a bitch," he pronounced contentedly. Afterwards, Roberta and the car met us. The city manager, who had escorted us down the steps of the town hall, was visibly staggered when Roberta, dressed in pea green to match the car, did a little curtsy and kissed my father on the cheek. An Edwardian tableau. I wondered if they had rehearsed it, or if, like experienced actors, they could simply improvise any scene.

On the drive home, my father said, "Stephen, are you really doing that retirement bit?"

These days he had fallen into the habit of using expressions that he considered hip. I found it annoying, but was especially careful not to say so. Nothing would encourage him more than my disapproval.

"Yes," I said, looking out the window. We were passing Dick Waltham's used-car lot.

"I simply cannot see you living anywhere else. You know every inch of this town. I imagine you have counted the cracks in the sidewalks."

"I thank you for your concern," I said stiffly. "But we, Lucy and I, have discussed this rationally. . . ."

He burst out laughing. So long and so hard that he gave himself a fit of coughing and we had to turn on the small tank of oxygen he carried for such emergencies.

¶ Everett Maley, my assistant pastor, was here a few moments ago. He wanted to ask about some small changes in the Sunday morning service. He is a capable man, no doubt. But sometimes I wonder if he will continue the work I have started here. Sometimes I am even tempted to stay on. It is an impulse I resist most firmly. I have planned my remaining years. First I will finish my study of Philo, which is very nearly complete. It's in my desk drawer, a stack of papers, neatly typed, footnotes numbered serially. After that, I will begin work on Plotinus. And after, Averroës.

I have always organized carefully.

Years ago I wrote out a detailed plan for my life—in the first volume of my journals. Those books there—do you see them? There are a dozen now, they fill an entire shelf, changing color and style occasionally over the years. They are all leather bound, and have something of dignity. . . .

I bought the first of them forty years ago in Philadelphia. (I've long ago forgotten why I was there.) I simply happened to pass a small bookseller's shop. I went inside, of course; I always do. It is quite impossible for me ever to pass a book-shop. Incidentally, I can also tell you where and when I bought each and every one of my books. Over there now, that set of Toynbee, that was Blackwell's in Oxford, the spring of 1930. It was one of the first copies sold. . . . I have such memories for every book on my shelves.

In the Philadelphia shop I bought a set of Dr. Johnson, the 1801 edition, in very good condition. (It's in the upstairs hall now, near the window. That curtain is always tightly drawn, of course. The light would ruin the bindings.) The bookshop was also a bindery. I ordered five blank volumes, morocco, eighteen inches high, no markings, gilt edged. On the first flawless white page I wrote *Journal, 1933, Stephen Henley.* At the top of the second page, I began carefully writing down a complete plan for my life. A timetable, as it were.

I have managed to keep quite closely to that schedule. Fur-thermore, over the years I have developed confidence in its authority and wisdom. At twenty I was more intelligent and more perceptive than at any other period of my life. Ideals are so easy to lose sight of—which is of course why I wrote everything down. I need to be reminded.

Shortly before we married, I showed the journals to Lucy. I did not want to enter into an agreement as serious as marriage without complete frankness. . . . As a matter of fact, my journal, though specific about many things—the order and title of every one of my books, beginning with the translation of Juvenal I published at twenty-two and continuing through the projects of my retirement, then forty years in the future—was very vague on the subject of marriage.

The only reference was under the general heading of my thirty-fifth year. By then I was to have completed my translation of Catullus into modern English poetry and "if not married this year, I am never to marry." As I explained to Lucy: "After that age a man becomes too accustomed to his solitude to adjust to the shared life of marriage." I think she understood. I am sure she did.

The very existence of this journal always amused my son Thomas. Why set up laws to tyrannize yourself? he'd say.

Over and over I would explain that rationality was not the same as tyranny.

"Thomas," I would say, "you need not agree with my principles. But why do you feel called upon to change my way of thinking in order to justify yours?"

He never answered my point.

Thomas acknowledged no interests but his own, and those he pursued vigorously. For example, he'd assembled an extraordinary collection of butterflies and moths. He'd started it as a second-grade science project, and he'd been working on it ever since.

One afternoon he was arguing with me, in his usual fashion: "Is this the year you translate the *Crito* or the *Phaedo?* And why the hell do you have to translate them at all? There are shelves of translations in the library."

"You looked!" I pretended surprise.

He threw himself into a chair.

"Careful," I said, "that might easily break. . . . But you asked a question. . . . Translations of the Greeks are almost without exception the work of nineteenth-century Englishmen. They are very Christianized. A fact that must amuse Plato considerably. I am trying to do a more accurate translation."

He threw up his hands in mock horror. "You always have a reason."

"A good reason," I said.

"Seriously now, Father, doesn't this fifty-year plan of yours seem just a little bit ridiculous?"

"More than your ten-year plan for the butterfly collection?"

"It's impossible to argue with you, Father. You are a complete sophist." I could hear his steps down the hall and out the back door. His butterfly collection was in the garage. He'd gone back to work on it.

Thomas has always been my favorite son.

At eight or nine, Paul reproached me for my attachment to his brother, and I found it a very good time to explain the entire situation. "You do like Thomas better than me," Paul complained.

"Yes," I said. I saw him start. Surprise, hurt. Children expect reassurance even when they know it false. "It is perfectly normal and natural for every person on this earth to have a favorite. Whenever there is more than one thing to consider, the human mind arranges an order of precedence. Do you follow me?"

He nodded. His yellow-brown eyes were watching me carefully.

"I like your mother more than any other woman. I like my pipe mixture better than any other. I prefer dachshunds to all other dogs. No human being can like things equally. I have two sons, therefore I must have a favorite."

The beginning gleam of a tear in his eye—he was not understanding me. I tried again.

"Paul, I have always been honest—most especially with people I love. And by the way, you know, though I prefer Thomas, that does not mean I don't love you a great deal."

The tear dried, the sparkle vanished. He sat perfectly still for a moment. You could feel distance coming between us. But with the coolness there was also understanding.

I told Lucy later: "There was nothing else I could do. I couldn't lie to him."

"He's little," Lucy said.

"Even very small children do not deserve lies."

"Yes," she said.

Which of course meant no.

¶ "The end of this year," Lucy said. "Christmas will be your last sermon." Her eyes were vague. You could almost see the clicking of file cards in her brain. All the things to be done. All the details.

Lucy's life has been lived with details. Perhaps there is comfort and warmth in them for her.

I myself dislike all such tedious housekeeping details, but I cannot completely avoid them. Take the matter of my books. There are nine thousand six hundred fifty-three books under this roof, and I can put my hand instantly on any one of them. I must pack them now myself, checking against my catalogue as I go.

¶ Since my twentieth year I have known that this Christmas would be my last sermon.

But now in November, now that I must write it, I am at a loss. I, who never once in my life had trouble putting my thoughts on paper, find that in the end, I have no suitable thoughts.

I wish that years ago, when I planned my life, I had also outlined this sermon. My young mind was so much more capable than the one I now possess.

My congregation will expect the usual Christmas message —of hope and peace and love. Of dignity and happiness. And a man who has lived as long as I—with some success, some happiness—should be able to write a Christmas sermon from his own depths of feeling. . . . I have written three drafts, but somehow the joyousness of birth eludes me, the sense of hope in darkness. I seem to dwell on the labor and the pain. My Bethlehem seems more like Calvary. My midwinter festival seems so bleak, in the dark of the year they are not lighting nearly enough bonfires. . . .

The fires again. I can't imagine why that one image returns to me so often.

It is a winter's day and very cold. There is no snow and the grass is still green, but the turf under my feet is frozen solid. The short day darkens. Then, the fires. Sparse at first, then steadily increasing. In a wide circle. Low flat prickles of light running like a brushfire along the ground. Climbing to tall peaked trees of light. And I stand quite alone in the middle of the yellow gleaming fires.

Should I include that in my sermon—my midwinter fires? I doubt it would make sense to my congregation. It hardly makes sense to me.

What I shall do, of course, is go back in my files, some twenty years or so, and revise an old sermon. I always write them out completely, and I always keep them neatly. A useful habit.

❡ I have been thinking about Lucy. My journal gave so little space to the selection of a wife, to her qualities. As if in my younger days she was of no importance to me.

That was a great oversight in my plan. (I was young, and I was not aware.) Lucy has been a comfort, a support. She has matured into a handsome woman, far more beautiful than when I married her. She is quiet, thoughtful, busy. And yet when she is out of the room, I have trouble remembering that she was ever within it.

She seems strangely shadowy to me, without substance.

I do not know what she thinks about so many things—or if she does. I do not know how she feels about so many things. Could she write a Christmas sermon? Would she too have to seek recourse in old thoughts?

❡ There is one thing missing from my plan. The date of my death.

Theoretically I should be able, by a combination of the

tangents of feeling and thought, to discern the intersection that equals death.

Perhaps I do have some indication. In my schedule of projected books I notice that I have planned nothing after my study of Maimonides and Averroës and the Judeo-Islamic world of Toledo. Did I stop because I could think of nothing more? Or because I preferred to leave this elderly man a last bit of freedom, unplanned, unscheduled? Or was it because as a young man I had sensed something? Some conjunction of forces said: This is the last, this is the end.

The spot where all but one line meets . . . when the next converges, the trap closes. The silence is permanent.

¶ Thinking like this, how can I help but talk of Calvary at Christmas?

I grow old. I grow old.

¶ My father came visiting. I heard the trained tinkle of Roberta's laughter. And a rattle of bottles as the heavy tread of his chauffeur moved through my hall.

Lucy called: "Stephen, your father is here."

My father, now, where is his point of intersecting lines? Does he feel their approach? Is he indifferent?

He appeared at my door, walking quite easily. For a while he had to use a wheelchair, but no longer. He has outlived even his illnesses.

He looked around my study, as he has done a thousand times, and his face indicated surprise and a touch of horror.

He found the room ugly. The plain board shelves, sagging with their weight of books. The rugs with neat round holes punched by years of pressure from the chair legs. The cross-braced oak table under the window, solid and enduring. (I bought it from a dentist's office the year I came to this church. The color has darkened considerably over the years, but the varnish has not lost its shine. It is almost like black lacquer.) The desk itself—very good English nineteenth-century mahogany—my father bought for me when I was a boy. Its leather top long ago wore to dust. I've covered it with two large green blotters. Once there were velvet curtains at the windows. They literally fell from their hooks some years ago, leaving the windows bare, except for pull shades.

My father crinkled his nose at the smell of dust and the faintly carbolic odor of bindings.

"By the way," he said, "I'm coming to your Christmas sermon, did I tell you?"

"I am very pleased." He had never come before.

"Thomas and Paul will be there too. Everyone will be home for Christmas." He grimaced at the phrase. "Dear Lord, how shabby! Oh yes, I'm giving you a party."

He tapped his cane against a shelf of books. (He carried that stick more for show than for use.) "Your farewell Christmas party."

"Father, please stop that. You're ruining the bindings."

He shrugged and turned. "I've taken over the Dawson Arms for that week."

"The Arms?" It was a small hotel, just outside town, in a pleasant open stretch of soybean fields.

"Roberta is turning it into an old English Christmas setting. Disgustingly maudlin. Everybody should love it. We'll need snow." He glared at me. "You arrange for snow. Pray for it."

¶ Now, in this last day of the final year of my ministry, I sit in my study again. Except for the steady pop, pop, pop of illegal New Year firecrackers outside, it is quite calm. My father's Christmas celebration is now safely past.

Vince Costello, my old friend from the Parks and Playgrounds Commission, just telephoned to say: "No one has ever had a more wonderful tribute than you've had right here."

He meant the events of Christmas Day. Everyone seems to share his feelings.

I am not sure I do.

¶ My father took over not only the Dawson Arms but the entire town as well. He'd always been generous, but this time he outdid himself. Using a great deal of money, Roberta produced the dazzling illusion of a nineteenth-century world.

Invitations to members of the church were written on heavy cream-colored paper and delivered by carriage and liveried footman. Those were, my wife said, the first-class invitations. I looked at her carefully to see if she was joking. She was not. "They deserve something special," she said, half to herself, "for standing by you all these years."

I was not aware that it had been so difficult.

The other invitations went by mail. They were written on blue or pink paper, according to their different functions.

Christmas morning service in the church was for the holders of those cream-colored cards. The blue invitations were for late afternoon at the Dawson Arms. The pink ones were for early evening. Lucy had found a way to avoid the impossible crush of having everyone at once.

The morning service was to be in period costume. I had not thought people would cooperate, but they did. Enthusiastically.

(I of course did not. I have worn the same suit every Sunday for the last fifteen years—my weight never changes—and I was determined to wear it once more.)

On the platform behind me sat my family, row on row. Roberta's fiery hair was partially hidden under a charming white cap. (She was there as a distant cousin, which people probably did not believe.) My father was in full maroon velvet with elaborate lace cuffs—powdered, wigged, subtly antique, a gentleman of the early eighteenth century. My sons, both in blue, Paul with a brown wig, Thomas with his own long hair clubbed into a black bow. Their wives, one mauve, one pink, their four children, three boys and a girl in shades of green, all velvets and satins.

Even the organ sounded different: a professional was playing today. The clear chords of the Bach Christmas cantata broadcast their message—*A voice calls us, awake!*

When I rose to take my accustomed place in the pulpit (the wood floor there was worn into the shape of my heels), I was very nearly unable to deliver my sermon. As I looked across the church, I felt a physical impact, a shock. Part of the effect was, of course, the lighting. The harsh overhead lights were gone. The entire hall gleamed softly with masses of electrified candle sconces. The hundreds of tiny flickering imitation flames produced exactly the wavering uncertain glow that belongs in old places and old books, the feel of another time that makes time uncertain.

The same subtly distorting lights brushed the edges of the building's solid functional walls and ceiling, softening their colors and their shapes.

And the congregation. Row after row of pews filled to capacity with costumed figures. Waiting for me to begin. Their faces were familiar. Most assuredly so. (I'd been seeing some of them for thirty-five years.) But somehow different—the difference a wig makes in a man, a prim housewife's ribboned bonnet in a woman. It was a little like looking at an ancestral portrait gallery. Except that these portraits breathed and snuffled and coughed in the expectant way of all audiences.

I did note that the costumes were a good bit earlier than they ought to have been. This church was built in the early 1840's; the costumes dated from the late 1700's. Roberta's history was not up to her theatrical flair.

That little incongruity enabled me to begin my sermon. And to finish it off creditably.

Which I did.

¶ After services we went to the Dawson Arms. Again Roberta had been at work. The building sparkled with warmth and charm like an illustration from a Dickens novel. Garlands of greens and flaming red ribbons, holly and ivy and mistletoe. Handsome livery for the servants, even including the small army of young men who parked cars. Waiters in knee breeches and stockings passed anachronistic martinis with silent efficiency. At two o'clock, we sat down to a huge mid-afternoon dinner. All my parishioners.

Outside the windows gleamed the blue light of new snow. Yes, it had snowed. My father had been gratified even in that.

For the athletic guests he'd constructed a huge skating rink. Beside it, on a heated terrace, a Bavarian band thumped away. In the dark trees, thousands of lights twinkled and flashed. The still, cold air was laced with sweet roasting chestnuts and the fiery trails of hot grog. At the barbecue pit, a haunch of beef waited, steaming. When the early winter dark fell, hundreds of yards of surrounding bare fields suddenly blazed with torches.

Thomas said, "It is incredible; that's the only word." His blue eyes danced with alcohol, his face flushed with the sudden extreme changes in temperature.

He was quite handsome, this son of mine. Not tall, but powerfully built. I could not see him spending hours with his microscopes and slides and minuscule bits of things.

"What do you think of my long hair?" he said.

"I assume you grew it just for the party."

He laughed, a short sharp bark. "Father, who's the girl standing behind you? Introduce me."

It was Anne Edwards, granddaughter of Lowell Edwards, the church treasurer. I had known Anne all her life and noticed her no more than any other eighteen-year-old in the congregation. Now, thanks to the strange twist of optics that costuming provides, she was startlingly beautiful. She wore a flowered dress, and her long dark hair was bound around her head like an Italian Madonna. Her slightly slanted dark eyes were openly appraising my son.

Some time later they were skating together—I saw them flashing in and out of the pools of yellow torchlight. Eventually I suppose they found their way to her parked car, one of those hundreds jamming the roadway and the lanes.

They did not return for almost two hours.

My father was very much amused.

Claudia, Thomas' wife, scarcely seemed to notice their absence. But then nothing excited Claudia. She was easygoing and casual to the point of sleepiness. "What does she do all day?" Lucy once asked me in rhetorical exasperation. Claudia had no job, no interests. Her housekeeping was appallingly chaotic. How often during the past ten years had Thomas telephoned: "We've got a mess again, Mother. How the hell can I work like this. . . . Can you come?" And Lucy, tight-lipped with annoyance, would go to Bloomington to house-clean and cook and organize the raveled threads of their ex-istence. Now, thank heavens, the frequency of those calls was steadily declining. Lucy had not been there for almost a year. Their two boys were growing up. They seemed in-creasingly able to manage the marketing and the cooking; with their father they conducted periodic cleaning blitzes. Claudia apparently did nothing at all. Strange. Before her marriage she'd been a tennis instructor at the university, a radiantly lovely girl with curly black hair and wide blue eyes. She was now a beautiful woman—one who either trusted her husband implicitly or was completely indifferent to him.

When next I saw Thomas, he was in the small taproom, singing carols with a group of five young women, his light clear baritone supporting their piping sopranos. The songs were quite appropriate, but their true meaning was not in their words.

My father, refreshed and alert after a nap, joined them, smiling beneficently across the length of the bar. Thomas smiled back at him, complacent and proud.

"Do you enjoy our singing, Grandfather?"

"Beautiful," my father said. "Please go on."

"With pleasure, Grandfather."

"There is," my father said to me later, "a definite odor of women in heat. Very definite."

"What?"

"In the taproom with Thomas," he said. "It was extremely strong."

¶ The earliest group, my parishioners, left. Exhausted by food and liquor, their costumes wilting, they drove off to their homes, first carefully lining up their rented wigs across the back car windows. The arriving groups were not in costume; but there were many more of them.

The mayor and the city council, all six of them, marched in together, as linked in life as their names were on public documents. The fire chief. The police chief. The president of the local Catholic college and four or five of his people, beaming and red-faced, over their swishing black robes. They brought a visiting red-robed monsignor. There were the town's two Medal of Honor winners. They had got out their dress uniforms and the real round-the-neck medals, not the ribbons.

And how people did congratulate Lucy and me! They congratulated us as if we had just given birth to the Christ Child. . . .

It was over about midnight. A crew appeared moments after the last guest and began extinguishing the torches and cleaning the litter. There seemed to be an inordinate number of broken glasses around the skating rink.

¶ And so it was that I finished my active ministry at a party presided over by an ancient man, while midwinter fires burned in circles, and alcohol-released people followed their sexual impulses.

It was everything my life had not been.

Curiously, not even the most conservative members of my congregation took offense. It was as if they had seen only what they wanted to see.

Though the odor of women in heat, as my father had said, was overpowering.

¶ In the dark of the early year, I finished the tedious work of packing up my life. There were last-minute crises. Simple church affairs suddenly became complicated. The mortgage must be renegotiated. The insurance coverage was deficient. Someone had lost the list of Sunday school teachers. The books I had given to the church library—two encyclopedias, a hundred or so volumes on various phases of humanistic philosophy—would I want them back?

Even Lucy's housework seemed terribly confused. "We will need so little," I asked her, "why not give away most of this?"

"Stephen, most of these things were presents, some even go back to our wedding. If I gave them away people would be hurt."

Lucy the perfect, Lucy the thoughtful. Lucy, who kept lists of wedding presents for thirty-four years. . . .

¶ Eventually we finished. While Lucy supervised the actual moving, I went to Washington for two months' work at the Library of Congress.

I walked out of my familiar house one morning and, after an interval spent in timeless concentration on uncomfortable chairs, I walked into a different house in a different world.

¶ How shall I describe Lucy's retirement haven, the dream house of her later years? The perfect place for us to advance, hand in hand, into golden senility.

On the flat sandy ground, thousands of insects—crickets and roaches and such—fled from hundreds of pursuing chameleons. In the clear hot air above the ground bright-colored dragonflies fed on mosquitoes. Swooping birds snapped up dragonfly and chameleon indiscriminately.

It was like living in the midst of a battle.

I can tolerate the insects of summer—brief things of a short life, a slightly extended mayfly world. But here, without the antiseptic sterility of freezing winter, insects grow in fantastic profusion. The big flying roaches with their gossamer wings seemed eons older than I and my species, as we both walked under the trees at dusk.

Lucy and I had slipped back in time. Our house was surrounded and protected by a magic white circle, a voodoo circle of malathion crystals carefully renewed each week.

These insecticides, which are everywhere, account for the sluggish condition of the insects. They do not die but they do not move in a lively fashion either, which may also account for the singularly ragged and sick look of the neighborhood cats. They feed on poisoned insects. They are so slow, these insects, so easy to catch, the cats probably cannot believe their luck.

"Do the cats know they are being poisoned?" I asked Lucy.

"Are they?" I explained; she shrugged. "I have to put out

insecticide or the house will be swarming. The cats will have to watch out for themselves."

So there it was. *Caveat emptor. Caveat feles.*

¶ My new study has two rooms. The study itself: my old desk (untouched), my old chairs (also untouched), a new rug of soft pinkish beige. The larger adjoining room, my library: crisscrossed by rows of gray steel library shelving; my books together in one place for the very first time in my life. The shelves were empty when I first saw them. (Lucy knew I would want no one to handle my books.) I walked up and down the narrow aisles dragging my fingers across the length of each shelf, tracing each one.

The small air-conditioner hummed a comforting monotone. The air moved slightly, not too much—perfect ventilation for the books. The floor underfoot was some sort of polished vinyl. My rubber-soled shoes squeaked very softly as they cushioned my aging spine against the shock of the hard tiles. The fluorescent tubes overhead buzzed like a far-off beehive.

Years ago I'd heard that same sound on my father's farm in Pennsylvania. I had a set of ponies—roans, I think—which I often drove across the pastures. There were hives in an adjoining field, lines of white boxes, and I often reined in to listen to the steaming hiss of the swarms.

I was dreaming like that when Thomas interrupted me. (He'd come down to check out the place, he said.) He stood in the doorway, his heavy figure reaching from post to post, his florid face gleaming with the heat of the tropical day.

"You're walking in circles, Pop," he said. "The sun get you?"

I tried to explain.

He nodded. "Yeah," he said. "Sure. Territory. You know. See it all the time with dogs. They pee their boundary markers, and when it smells of them, then they're happy. You been peeing in the corners, Pop?"

Seeing the annoyance in my face, he said, "Oh come on, Pop, I'm joking."

Territory indeed. Still I must admit that I was no longer quite so pleased with the shelving.

¶ My study was actually a separate building, connected to the rest of the house by a short screened walkway. It was entirely my world, and I immediately set about making some changes in it. I disliked the wide windows; I found the shimmering tropical light disquieting and deceptive. Its glaring white dazzle persisted even through the late afternoons until its abrupt extinction by nightfall.

I drew the curtains and worked by electric light. In the dry air-conditioned coolness I was insulated and completely apart.

The house itself was not air-conditioned; it was ventilated by a series of louvers in the doors, in the windows, in the walls, in the roof—all controlled by handles or pulleys or chains. There was even an awning over the patio that lifted at the buzz of an electric motor.

The house seemed—how shall I say?—a mechanical house. It ran like a wind-up toy.

"It's like a greenhouse," Lucy explained.

I had noticed the similarity.

Long ago, my father and Eleanor built a greenhouse for me, a monstrous thing, very much like those glass palaces the

Victorians favored—with a touch of Brighton added. All the upright steel beams blossomed into sprays of pineapple leaves just before they reached the roof. They were gilded, those leaves, but the humidity soon stripped them in a shower of gold flakes. Within those glass walls grew a carefully approximated jungle of palms and bananas and strange flowering trees and broad-leafed plants (all labeled with the proper Latin names) whose leaves ran water incessantly, like very small trickling streams. There were three parrots, a macaw, and brilliant flocks of smaller birds. There was even a pair of monkeys. The thermometer proved that they were quite warm, but the poor things still shivered all through the long gray winters. They didn't swing from branch to branch, or chatter. They sat huddled among the gold-flaking iron leaves at the very top of the roof, hunched and miserable. They were comfortable enough, but perhaps they missed the sunlight.

I'm sure that the jungle was Eleanor's idea. My father's ways of amusing me were much more ingenious.

When animals no longer interested me, my father thought of the ultimate pet: another human.

One day, a boy my own age appeared, to live in my house. He was mine to play with, to study. The first was Chinese, the second Indian, the third Negro. All exotics. Of course. A toy must be highly colored to attract a child's eye.

They stayed with us for weeks or months, those children; when I tired of them, they were replaced by another pet human.

It was a clever way to amuse a lonely boy.

I outgrew even those toys. I discovered books and spoke of an interest in Latin. My father at once produced a retired Jesuit, who moved into the house to become my tutor. (My father said that he had borrowed him from his college. Which, I suppose, meant that he gave a large amount of money to their fund. That was always my father's way of getting things done.) With this immensely learned man, I entered a world I had not known existed. A world I have never left.

Father David Harold Lawrence had short gray hair that must once have been blond and thick glasses and pale-blue eyes like little marbles in a casting cup in some obscure game. I looked down a contracting cone at him, he looked back through a widening flare. . . .

Despite those lenses he did not see very well. He held books to his nose and squinted, reading hour after hour in that painful way. Impelled, driven by love of each succeeding word, by the great mystery of each following page. . . . He's been dead these many years of course. It seems to me sometimes that I know more of the dead than of the living. Another fancy of mine: when that really becomes true, when the weight of the dead in my memory exceeds the numbers of living I deal with daily, then the balance will tip. And I join the silent majority.

Father Lawrence was with me for, I suppose, two years. Why do I remember him now?

A sign of senility, they say, when early memories become more vivid than recent ones. As if the human organism were altering its forward flight through time, as if it were reversing its passage to travel back through childhood to the womb. To the final nothingness of the unborn.

It lingers in my mind, that forward-and-back motion of human life. Somewhat like a railroad siding whose switches are never opened. If it had only been a circle, you would have the illusion of progress. . . .

But, Father Lawrence. He told me, in practically the only personal conversation we ever had (mostly he tried to impress on me the beauties of Cicero's periods), that he was an Irishman. That he still remembered the rainy green slopes where children ran freely as little animals, stopping now and then to stare reverently at certain high patches of grass in the pastures. Wherever a famine victim fell, he told me, forever after the grass grew ranker than in other spots.

On that dark Pennsylvania afternoon with the lead-colored snowy sky tight around our heads, I thought about Ireland and its memorials of rank grass that grazing animals refused to touch.

The idea was interesting. In a reversal of values, the living became a memorial to the dead. A pity that the story could not be true. . . .

I told him, "If grass grew tall wherever a man died, there wouldn't be room for anything else. Down toward the river, at the edge of the croquet lawns, there was a fort once and Indians attacked it and people got killed. That's all lawn now, no special tufts of grass."

"That was murder." He polished his glasses calmly. "In Ireland it was famine."

We went back to Cicero. I sulked all the rest of the afternoon because he seemed illogical to me. . . . Now I am not so sure.

¶ All day long, in the blazing Florida light, Lucy opened louvers, drew blinds, lowered awnings. The house required constant adjustment to the climate, to the sun that burns and cracks and fades. Lucy seemed to delight in these varied stratagems against an external enemy.

I felt embattled. My curtains stayed drawn, my windows closed. But cool dry air flowed from my window unit. And my work on Plotinus and the Neo-Platonists progressed very nicely.

Just exactly as I had planned.

And Lucy—well, Lucy, as always, was tireless. We had not been here a month before she became secretary of a newly organized Unitarian Fellowship. Even before that she'd volunteered to work three mornings a week at the admissions desk of the county hospital. She began to play golf. And to go to transcendental meditation classes. "Great nonsense," she called them.

"Why go then?"

"Because I might be wrong."

I myself stayed home, working quietly, until the small Jesuit college in nearby Lake Park called me. They needed someone to teach Greek. Four freshmen had requested it, and the good fathers had forgotten the fruits of their seminary training.

I accepted. I rather enjoyed the idea of rendering back unto Caesar the things that had come from him in the first place. I could return to Father Lawrence's order the knowledge that he had lent me half a century before. Quite a long-term loan, you might say.

¶ One afternoon—the usual blazing white day—I sat behind drawn curtains in my study. The desk chair squeaked each time I moved—exactly the way it had done for thirty years. On the shelf directly across from me were the volumes of my journal. The years were there, in the progression of gold numbers on the spines.

It was a bit like watching sand fall in an hourglass. You could actually see the passage of time.

I am sixty-one, I thought. My father is ninety-one, and my mother is. . . .

I had to stop. I didn't know. The woman I thought of as my mother, Eleanor Halsey, had only been my father's wife.

My situation had always seemed simple: I was my father's son, subsequently adopted and legitimized. My natural mother had incubated me for my father in much the same way she would have made a shirt or woven a rug or stitched a quilt—or any other project requiring considerable time and care. Her product had been found satisfactory, she had been well paid. (My father was never miserly.) If I ever doubted my paternity, there was my strong resemblance to my father to convince me.

I rarely thought of my beginnings. It was—how can I explain it?—like having red hair. Somewhat unusual, but not important.

Now—the journals with their careful markings of the years, the irresistible progression of numbers—I began to think.

Eleanor, that kindly stupid woman with the comfortable flesh of a cow. She loved me, she loved everything, even a stray pup without a tail. She rescued him from drowning one afternoon at the Wisset River. (In his old age he abruptly grew something that passed for a tail, a bony, partially fur-covered appendage.) She mated him with a black-and-white female, thinking I suppose to start a line of tailless dogs. The pups were perfectly normal, but she loved them anyway. . . . She loved plants too. In her last apartment, three rooms high in the east corner of the Ritz Hotel in Boston, she had one window filled with potted plants, renewed regularly and discreetly by her maid-companions. Poor Eleanor, she never seemed to notice that the blazing tree azalea was always in the same state of bloom. She had moved into a world where flowers were permanently fixed to branches, where tulip cups were always erect and dusted with the first opening pollen.

Eleanor remained my mother, while my father had his progression of women and, unfortunately, an occasional man.

But now, I wondered: What had that other one been like? I possessed a strong resemblance to my father of course, but something of her must show in me.

It was annoying.

My father had no idea what became of her. It was like my father to have no interest in a thing after its usefulness for him was past.

It was annoying.

There was a pencil near my fingers. I tossed it point first at the journals, whose numbers had started this intolerable train of thought. I missed.

I tried again—there was a low cup filled with pencils, like flowers, on the corner of my desk. And again. One reached the books, eraser first. It hit with a soft rubber thud, a tiny smudgy sound.

I changed my technique. I began balancing the pencils on my index finger and flipping them, end over end. They flew wildly, hitting the bookshelves, the curtains, the lamp.

When Lucy walked in, I was down to my last pencil and the floor was littered with bits of yellow and red and green.

She said quietly, "Dinner is ready, if you're finished."

I stood up, a bit hastily so that my arthritic back gave a

twinge. "Uuf," I said, not meaning to have said anything. And then, "I'll just pick these up, Lucy, and then I'll be right along."

I began picking them up very slowly, bending gingerly from the waist.

"I'll help." She crouched down and began gathering handfuls.

"Lucy," I said, "I don't want you to think this is irrational behavior."

She stood up, herself a bit slow, and put the pencils back into the container. "I am sure you have your reasons, Stephen. I would never call you irrational."

While we both stood rubbing our creaking backs (her ache was lower than mine, more nearly a true sciatica), I explained to her how my unknown mother had disturbed the plan of my day.

As I went on, I noticed a very strange expression on Lucy's face. It was—how shall I describe it?—a bit like that of a child with a secret.

¶ Shortly afterwards Lucy insisted that we visit Paul and Jane.

"There's no need," I argued. "They come here twice a year. I don't like Chicago and I hate to travel; you know that."

"They have such a lovely apartment," Lucy said. "You must see it. It's a Mies van der Rohe building."

"I'm hardly interested in architecture, Lucy." But she would not listen.

Actually, once we started, once the house door was locked behind us, I began to look forward to the visit. I had always felt a certain hesitancy in our relationship with Paul. Perhaps because he was younger, he had more illnesses than his brother: sore throats, rheumatic fever, pneumonia. He was a quiet child, intelligent and extremely well organized. Most often he simply informed you of plans he had already worked out. (Thomas, on the other hand, always began with half-realized ideas and developed them in conversations with you.) At thirteen he'd asked about boarding school: "Father, do you think you can afford it?" It was really not a question at all. He'd already selected the school, had been in touch with the admissions people, had made all arrangements, including financing—in case his mother and I should not be able to find the money.

As I said before, he always reached his conclusions alone.

And his wife, Jane—I found even more certainty there. She was small and pretty and looked far younger than her actual age. She'd dropped out of medical school to marry Paul. And she still seemed to carry some of that clinical atmosphere with her. Though she was unfailingly kind and reassuring, I found something disturbing in her almost professional solicitude.

I mentioned this to Lucy, who shrugged: "She and Paul appear happy together."

"Don't you wonder what she is really like? What she thinks?"

"She thinks exactly what every nearly middle-aged mother of two children thinks."

"What's that?"

"Nothing at all," Lucy said.

¶ The flight to Chicago was unusually tiring for me. By the time Lucy and I walked into the crowded concourse, I could not see clearly at all. No problem with my glasses. My wearying eyes, with increasing frequency, were playing tricks like this. They bounced along the edges of things, taking in lights and reflections and shapes and colors. And not the meaning at all.

More or less like running your hand over a piece of wood. Concerned only with the surface polish, the curves, the faint grain. Not thinking about what it was, a chair or a table or a desk. . . .

This growing habit of mine, this non-focusing, began a few years ago during my sermons. The audience, which since our student days we had been taught to regard as a set of individuals, would sometimes blur into neat lines of smooth egg shapes. Then even the eggs would lose their identities and I would be speaking to a canvas of colored smears.

Luckily my eyes were not always that unreliable. I had also discovered that food helped me to focus. I carried a piece of cheese in my pocket for just such a purpose.

¶ Paul's apartment was very high, I forget exactly which floor. The sway, which I always feel in tall buildings and which engineers have assured me means nothing at all, was very noticeable. Most unpleasant, most uncomfortable for me. I balanced carefully, putting my weight on the balls of my feet. When I sat, I braced my arms against the chair.

I disliked everything I saw: the white walls, the black steel-and-chrome furniture, the bowls of red flowers like blotches of blood, the endless dazzling windows. My light-sensitive glasses immediately began to darken. The whole apartment glared at you—everything was shiny as their collection of mercury glass.

"Your father sent it." Jane pointed to the brilliant shapes in their lighted cabinets. "Some of the pieces are really extraordinary."

"I believe his mother collected them," I said. "I seem to have heard that."

"*His* mother," Paul mocked me. "No connection of yours, I suppose."

"She would naturally be my grandmother," I said stiffly. I was not in a humorous mood. I had just discovered that the building's sway produced a detectable surge in the decanter on the coffee table.

"It all arrived one day," Jane said. "Box after box, I can't tell you how many. And a note saying: 'I think you'll like this.'"

"That is his manner," I said.

"Like the silver bowl he sent you, the one that looked like an old-fashioned foot tub," Lucy said.

"I thought it rather handsome," I said. "I thought it quite handsome."

"Where are the children?" Lucy changed the subject not very subtly.

"Dancing class," Jane said, "every Saturday morning."

"They won't be home before one." Paul put down a tray with two pitchers, one white, one red. "Milk punch or Bloody Mary?"

Jane said, "Paul has a dreadful hangover."

"You look quite healthy," I said. "Except you're beginning to gray."

He fingered the streaks; he knew just where to touch. He had done it before, patted that whitening patch of hair. "We grow old, Father, even your baby boy."

The wind mewed and rattled around the windows. The ice

in the Bloody Mary pitcher clinked softly. My senses registered the sway methodically, monitoring it.

"What would you do in a fire?" I asked Paul. "You're far beyond the reach of firefighting equipment."

"I suppose we'd be cooked like a roast," he said. "Or maybe smoked like a ham. Depending on the kind of fire."

Lucy said: "That is not funny."

"Don't worry," Jane said, "the only fires here are occasional ones in the janitors' closets."

Lucy said, "Aren't you even going to mention your other collection?"

Dutifully I asked: "What collection?"

"Paul's been accumulating the work of one artist for the last five or six years," Jane said. "We finally got enough to hang. You know, it takes quite a few to make an impression on these walls."

Paul filled his glass with the watery remains in the Bloody Mary pitcher. "We've hung them in the dining room, Father. Come see."

In the dining room the curtains were open. Beyond the floor-to-ceiling glass was a bit of dull-mirror lake, and an enormous jumble of Chicago streets, stretching off into the blue distance. That smoggy prairie—I found myself wondering what was out there. An explorer's thought: Beyond the horizon, what?

I stared—like a child's kaleidoscope, the pattern of color and shape and light changed, fluttered, shifted.

Directly in front of this immensity was a small bronze angel on a slender Plexiglas stand. Wings out, it flew over the abyss. Small and frozen and dwarfed against the sprawl of Midwest America.

"What's that?"

"Sixteenth-century Italian. Supposedly. Jane bought it a couple of months ago. Father, the pictures are here."

There were at least a dozen, none of them larger than twenty-four inches, all square rather than rectangular. Daylight glared from their high varnish—until Paul closed the curtains and turned on the soft electric lights. Because Paul valued them so highly (Paul, who was so careful with money), I studied them closely.

They were primitives. American. Rather good of their sort. The colors were clear, and there were a great many variations and shadings, not just the usual red, blue, and yellow palette.

"Not a true primitive," I said to Paul. "The colors are too studied and sophisticated."

"Good for you, Father." As if I had scored a point in a game.

Actually the clear bright color was the only interesting aspect—the subject matter, the technique were quite conventional. There were portraits, most with dark backgrounds in the fashionable manner of the last century; two of children had light yellow backgrounds; and one of an old woman displayed her drab brown dress against a pale green background. In a corner of that one floated an outsized monarch butterfly.

"Why the butterfly?"

"I asked," Paul said. "She didn't remember but she supposed she must have felt light as a butterfly that day. It's a self-portrait," he added.

"What was her name?"

"Mary Morrison Remick."

The other pictures. City streets, gray houses. Sometimes the plane trees were in leaf. Sometimes the branches were

bare and the sidewalks filled with bits of yellow. . . . Parks
and playgrounds of seventy years ago—girls with hoops and
boys with boats, and wicker governess carts rolling along the
gravel paths.

"She was partially trained," I told Paul. "Just look at the
horses. Somebody had to teach her to see horses like that."

"When she lived in Pittsburgh, when she was very young,
she studied with a man named Johnson. Do you know of
him?"

"No," I said. "And there's far too much varnish on all of
them."

"He was a teacher of considerable reputation some sixty
years ago. And I know the varnish is bad, but she wanted it.
She wanted to preserve her paintings."

"Johnson should have taught her better."

"She wasn't with him more than a year. Then she moved
to Minneapolis."

Dear, dear, how involved the boy was.

"She studied at the Art Institute in Minneapolis," Paul
went on. I was going to get the entire story of the painter's
life. "Then she married, he was a shop foreman, a good kind
hardworking German, and they had two children. She kept
on painting and eventually had quite a local reputation as
a portrait painter."

Paul rubbed away an invisible smear on his glass-and-
chrome dining table. Even in the soft artificial light the
room glittered harshly, jarringly. I understood why my father
had sent them the mercury glass. . . .

But I must be polite and show an interest in his dull paintings. "How many do you have?"

"Sixteen, Father."

One portrait hung a bit apart from the others, as if to emphasize its slightly different style. This was a young woman, her hair drawn back severely from a center part, tiny coral earrings in her ears, hands folded primly in her lap. She was wearing a silvery blue dress, with a high lace collar, tucks fanning across her shoulders like a sunburst. Her face was gentle and kind and placid, holding neither joy nor sorrow.

"Now that's been reproduced somewhere," I said. "I've seen that before."

"I thought so too," Paul said, "when I first saw it."

"It's been on a calendar. Or some such place. Wherever a touch of Americana would be the thing to have."

"It's very familiar," Paul repeated. "But it's never been reproduced."

"Oh, it must have. I'm certain I've seen it."

"No."

"There's another possibility. It's an adaptation of a famous picture and I'm seeing echoes of the original. Something like that."

I turned to the Italian angel. While I touched the graceful bronze wings, Paul remained staring at the small portrait.

"It's a quite good likeness," he persisted. "She was a very old woman when I met her, but I could tell that she must have looked just this way once."

"Interesting." I opened the curtains to have another look at the center of the United States.

"She put a house and a street in this picture."

(How tiresome the boy was!)

"Primitives often do that," I said. "It's really quite usual."

"Really, Father, look at this." He put the painting on the glass top of the dining table. "Here."

Floating disembodied in the portrait's upper right corner was a tall narrow brick house, and a bit of street outside its door. Paul took a magnifying glass from his jacket pocket. (When had he started behaving like an amateur Sherlock Holmes?) "She must have used a glass like this and a tiny almost single-hair brush—look."

The detail was fantastic. No doubt of that.

"The nearest I've been to this," I said, hoping to be mildly amusing, "was a grain of rice with the Lord's Prayer on it."

"Look at the doorway," Paul said. "Look at the corbels. Those are horses' heads."

"Yes, I suppose they are." Two tiny but unmistakable elongated equine heads.

Paul straightened up triumphantly. "It isn't just the house," he said. "There were hundreds like that built in the 1880's and 1890's. But did you ever see one with horses' heads on the corbels?"

"Paul, please. I just don't share your interest in primitive art, and I can't match your enthusiasm for late-nineteenth-century architecture."

His pecan-colored eyes danced with excitement. "Think where horse-head corbels were, Father."

I hesitated.

"Grandfather's house on Howland Street. You lived there for years. And I've seen the photographs." He was speaking very slowly and with great emphasis. "That is Grandfather's house. The way it looked years ago, about the time you were born. The potted plants on the steps, the tree on the left, and, of course, the foolish carvings on the corbels. I've studied those old photographs very, very carefully. This is the same house."

I looked again. Vague childhood memories did seem to confirm his statement.

"That's the way the house looked about the time you were

born," Paul said. "And do you know why her portrait looks familiar to you? That's yourself you're seeing. That's your mother."

I blinked.

"Look at it."

I sat down, propping the small piece of canvas against the flower-filled silver centerpiece. Red anemones peeped around the frame.

"Well, Paul, I suppose that is possible."

"So you see, she was all right after all. She was a talented painter, she had a fine family, and they all did very well. She wasn't hurt by you."

Hurt by me? I had never thought of it that way. . . . "I hardly think bearing a single child could hurt a healthy young woman, Paul."

"But giving him up. . . ."

I became impatient. "When it is possible to have many more children, one is not so important. There is a story of Catherine Sforza on the ramparts of Bologna, when the city was under siege and the enemy held two of her children as hostages. . . ."

"I know the story, Father."

"Do you? Paul, you are remarkably well read."

"You aren't interested, Father!"

It was a cry of pain. No less. From a thirty-three-year-old man. My stomach lurched.

"Yes," I said as gently as I could. "She *has* been in my mind this last year. Now that I'm nearing the end of my life, I seem to want to go back and pick up all the pieces and fit them together. . . . If you keep any brandy, we might have some." He got the bottle and two glasses silently, and pulled out the chair next to mine.

Eager. He was so eager.

I would just have to keep asking questions, until his enthusiasm ran its course.

"Did you meet her, Paul?"

He began a long account of his trip to Minneapolis, after he had seen some of her paintings in a regional show at the University of Chicago.

"Her works are very consistent, Father," he insisted, as if I were arguing. "They are strongly marked by a quite unique style."

"But how did you first identify the style, Paul?"

"It wasn't the style, really," he admitted. "But in that first show, she had nothing but portraits of boys—and they all looked a great deal like you."

"You mean they looked like *her*."

"And therefore like you, Father. You look less and less like Grandfather as you grow older."

"And more and more like her?"

He nodded. As he poured the brandy, his hand trembled. Poor Paul.

Was the presence of blood so important to him? What strange evidence of love was this?

"She is dead?" He nodded. I sipped at the brandy. It is one of the few spirits I truly like, and Paul's brandy was very good indeed. "Do you think there is some undefined community of blood, Paul? Her death stirred our kinship?"

How can I say this? I was bored. Even if the woman *were* my mother, well, it was not so important as all this.

Not to me. My recent concern with her was merely the instinctive neatness of an organized man. No more. There were no mentions of her in my journals. She had never figured in my life, except as that initial incubator. That I thought of her again was simply an indication I was considering my own mortality. I probably was thinking of my own tombstone: Stephen Henley, son of Edward Henley and . . . who? That is the only reason I thought of her, even casually.

I was, you must understand, rather glad to hear about her. To know who she had been—if indeed this was she. (Let it be this way. She will serve as well as any other. She henceforth will *be* my mother.)

I myself poured a second brandy. My hand, I noticed with pleasure, was absolutely steady. "I shall regret this all day," I told Paul. "I am not at all used to alcohol in the mornings."

"We conspire in your corruption," he muttered. He was annoyed with me, annoyed that I did not display a vital interest in his discovery. But how could I have changed the truth?

"Mother said you'd be interested."

Lucy had said that? I remembered: in the study she had come upon me idly tossing pencils at the volumes of my journal, meditating on the periodicity evident in human life. And she had misunderstood.

"Even your mother can be wrong," I said quietly.

He started to answer, then fell silent, looking down at his hands outstretched on the glass tabletop. He had an empty stubborn look—meaning that things were not going the way he expected. Lack of understanding had always made Paul sulky.

My own lack of understanding grows each year. Soon it shall be perfect and complete.

"But you haven't finished, Paul. You were telling me about meeting her in Minneapolis. Mrs. Remick, I mean. . . ."

His brown eyes clouded briefly. What was the matter? Did he actually expect me to call her mother?

On such short acquaintance? My dead mother. My long-lost mother. Have I found you at last? And it doesn't matter in the least to me.

I chuckled. Out loud.

Paul popped out of his chair as if an alarm bell had rung.

He always looks older when he is angry. His smooth soft face hardens into drooping curves. Becomes the sagging face of an old man. That is the way he will look when he reaches my age. . . . If I had a photograph of him now I would display it next to the self-portrait of his newly appointed grandmother. And I would call them: past and future. Prophecies of both. . . .

Or some such nonsense.

"The ladies will be waiting for us," Paul said formally.

I looked again at the small portrait on the table before me. There was a resemblance, certainly, but a great many Irish faces look alike. Years ago, when I traveled through that country, I noticed that whole towns looked enough alike to be cousins—as they probably were.

"Still," I said, continuing my thought, "it is a charming portrait, and a charming collection—all the more in this room of steel and glass. And if she is indeed a relative"—I looked into Paul's tense face—"all the better for us."

"It's taken me six years to collect these," he said, tentatively checking my interest. "The people who owned them didn't want to sell. And I didn't dare go see her at first. I suppose she heard about me, she could hardly avoid it. I had half a dozen agents, we even used newspaper ads. Some of that activity must have reached her. Anyway, three years ago, I went to see her. She was a very old woman, with dropsy or something like that. Her breath was very weak and it was hard for her to talk." He paused, as if he too had run out of breath. "She gave me this self-portrait, the one with Grand-father's house in the background."

She knew you were interested in her paintings, I started to say. Why not stop at that?

But I didn't say it aloud. Paul had invested so much in this, so much time and feeling—who was I to deny him his inter-pretation?

I stood up. "You seem to have found a grandmother," I said, in what I hoped was a light careless tone.

Paul's face began to shiver, literally to *shiver.* I thought: Dear Lord, he *is* going to cry. . . .

But the moment passed. And he only picked up the pic-ture and hung it back on the wall.

Then we did indeed join the ladies.

And that, you might say, was how I found and lost my mother. If that were my mother.

We mentioned it no more. It was as if it had never hap-pened. No. It *wasn't* quite like that. It was like a completed puzzle. Once you fit the last piece, you no longer need think about shape and form and color. You can even throw the whole puzzle away.

It was very much like that.

¶ Lucy and I returned to Florida.

I resumed my studies of Plotinus and the Neo-Platonists. I was progressing quite rapidly—my notes were almost com-plete.

I know that it is customary to laugh at the scholar. A man without pleasure. A man without blood. Without interest or substance.

How can I explain? How can I tell you the excitement of

the pursuit of an idea? The shimmering gossamer quality of words whose meanings have been waiting for hundreds of years. The soft sensuous smell of the books themselves. The slight rustle of slowly turning pages. The sound of each book is different, the size of the pages, the quality of the paper. The way the words appear on the page, the groupings, the shapes, the forms of the letters. . . . Not only mathematicians can speak of beautiful proofs. . . . The shape of words is beautiful, their balance, their symmetry or angularity is pleasing.

The ideas themselves, as they emerge from the shadows behind the words. . . . The beautiful ideas, how varied they are, how differently they comport themselves. How fascinating their individual revealings. . . . Some sidle seductively from their hiding places, some sulk and peer and never quite emerge. Some stand behind a window with a half-drawn curtain, frankly but partially visible.

Working, I sit surrounded by them, and the room seems quite crowded. And then I think I understand what a desert king felt in his harem. . . .

Don't misunderstand me. I don't see the ideas as female. I don't see them as human at all. It's just that they exhibit rather human traits.

It is, I suppose, an obscure infatuation, this seduction by the book. Like any other addiction it is extremely hard to explain. If I could hold in my hand, if I could possess, say, a Wycliffe Bible, I would be beside myself with joy. I have stared at that book through glass cages in museums and I have always felt an increase in heartbeat, a shortness of breath, the beginning of overwhelming excitement. If I could hold that book in my hand . . . the book that men died for. The actual physical book. Not a copy, not merely the words. But the thing itself. Who, during its long life, held it in their hands and studied the riddle of its words? Who turned its pages in the secrecy of shuttered rooms, knowing that its possession meant death? Do some of their emotions linger in the pages, is there a tinge, a coloration, a relic of their need to know, to think, a desire that meant more than life? Would there be left a tiny pulse of their determined blood, would there be a tremor of their fear and dread? . . . If I placed my fingers in the exact spot those fingers touched, would their terror and curiosity and hope—just a breath, just a touch— would it reach to me?

I am sure it would.

That is the only immortality I believe in. The linkage of understandable human feelings.

Of course, I never shall possess such a book. I shall have to make do with those photocopies that so nicely reproduce the shape but not the soul.

Once, when I was young, when my obsession was also young and therefore much less subject to control, I thought of asking my father to help me arrange to steal such a book. Just so. He would have had to put out a great deal of money, but I'm sure he would have, and gladly. Piratical ideas amused him greatly. (My father has a horror of being bored.)

I myself was deadly serious. It was the one truly larcenous plan of my life. I had the means, the desire. The way was open. I really do not know what stopped me. I think I was afraid that some unplanned violence would engulf the book itself. Or the haze of emotions that clung to it. I could not risk damaging either. It was, I suppose, a matter of love.

Now, each morning, I am so very eager to get to my study. I cannot wait to close the door behind me, to feel the shifting and shivering in the air, the murmur from the library stacks. There is no sensation when the door is open, and all

motion stops the instant another person enters the room. I
think I know why. These are my thoughts, my responses. The
movement of any other body interrupts them and they fall
broken to the ground.

I therefore am quite annoyed when anyone approaches me.
I find the sudden silent emptiness very disheartening.

Lucy knows this and almost never comes into the study.

She herself of course remains quite busy. Presently she
serves on the school board, the library board. She is now
president of the Unitarian Fellowship. She is also campaigning for a seat on the town council—the election will be in
November. She has added tennis to golf in her athletic program. The tropical sun does not seem to bother her at all.
She looks incredibly healthy. Were she a child, I would
almost certainly say: How you have grown! She gives the
impression of having added three inches to her already considerable height.

She is always home for my lunch. She is a good and clever
cook: she sees that my meals are on time and that they do not
upset my delicate metabolism. After lunch three days a week
I drive her to the public library, where she teaches a class of
dyslexic children. She is very good with them and their faces
show it—bright and eager. Sometimes, when I pick her up,
I come into the library. I usually wait at the corner window,
overlooking the garden where her class meets. I am quite content there, in the broken leather armchair. The room is rather
dusty, slow spinning motes in panels of sunlight. It is cool and
rather pleasant, its smell a mixture of paper and binding cloth
and sweat. The last time I was there, a child said to Lucy,
"He's waiting for you." "Well then"—she did not turn her
head—"I suppose we had better finish this page and stop."

Only He—deprived of my name I felt I was not really

present. As if any other person might just as easily have filled my seat at the window. Some other He. . . .

Lucy was flushed and happy as usual. "The children are so wonderful."

"A pity we only had two."

"I would have liked more," Lucy said.

"Would you?" I myself was quite content with the two boys. They fitted so nicely into the house. Though I suppose we might have found a larger house.

"I would have liked six," Lucy said with a wry grin, "if they had paid clergymen more liberally."

"I didn't know that."

"We never talked about it," she said, "because we had all the children we could afford."

"Well," I said, "well."

As we walked out of the library, Lucy slipped her hand into mine. And said with what was as close as Lucy ever got to humor: "The things you find out in your old age, Stephen."

¶ Ah yes. The changes of old age. I who had been so dutifully sociable, who had, during the days of my active ministry, been out every single night, visiting the sick, serving on committees, or dining with friends—I who had done that for thirty-five years with gusto and enthusiasm—I now found myself unwilling to step outside after dark.

How rapidly the feeling grew. I became decidedly uncomfortable at the approach of sundown. I disliked the slightest shadow falling on me. As if night were a stain that would soil me.

At first I made excuses. Then I no longer did. I told the simple truth, "I don't like to go out after dark."

The changes of old age. Yes, indeed.

Evenings Lucy and I watched television news and had supper. Then we sat together in the living room. I had a book from my library. She had her needlework. She was making a very large wall hanging of a knight on a prancing horse.

"Is it St. George?"

"No dragon," she said. "It can't be St. George."

Inch by inch the design crept forward. The animal's rear hoofs began to take shape. I am sure I would not have had the patience to work so slowly, in and out, each needle stroke positioned so exactly. The thread made a tiny hissing sound through the buckram. That small sound was characteristic of my evenings—methodical, evenly spaced, repetitious.

My dislike of the dark increased. I began bringing at least two books into the living room, because I could no longer bear to cross the fifty feet of floodlit breezeway to my study. Once I reached the safety of the house I would not leave until morning.

And even more. Like all Florida houses ours has large sliding glass doors in every room. Including of course the living room, which in our house was uncurtained because it opened onto a sheltered patio. Evenings I found myself watching that door—dark comes so quickly here, there is no twilight in this latitude, only a quick change from day to night.

When the entire room—with Lucy and myself in our chairs—was projected into the black, I became very nervous. I did not want even my reflection to be out there in the night.

Lucy made curtains. Until they were ready, I covered the glass with pieces of newspapers held in place by cellophane tape.

Lucy often went to meetings several nights a week. Without her the house seemed empty and quiet; I was especially glad of the security of the curtains.

I even began to enjoy these evenings alone. My thoughts moved more easily, more clearly. I was able to formulate new philosophical problems, to postulate new answers. I was able to consider my own position and the chain of events that had brought me to Florida.

¶ Thursday, the twelfth of August, Lucy went to a meeting of the library committee. I was not feeling well. I, who usually have a hearty appetite, had barely touched my supper. I had not said anything, lest Lucy be obliged to stay home with me. I was not sick, just vaguely uncomfortable.

Reading was difficult, but I persisted. After all, what is there for a scholar who cannot read? I held my book firmly and leaned closer to the lamp. As I did so, the lamp blinked. Once, twice. Annoyed, I reached for the flashlight we kept under the table. Power failures were not unusual here. The lights flickered again, then went out. What a miserable evening this would be. I snapped on the flashlight and continued my reading. It was a considerable strain on my eyes, and I blinked constantly.

Also, things seemed unusually quiet. During these blackouts, we always heard loud complaints from our neighbors as they bumbled about. Mr. Hazard, the gentleman whose lot adjoins ours, has a particularly penetrating voice and a remarkable variety of curses, both in English and Spanish. I ought to have heard him. I opened every one of Lucy's new curtains. It was completely dark outside. Strange. The Parkers, who live across the street, have an emergency generator; they at least should have light.

But I saw nothing. Nothing but emptiness and silence.

Perhaps they were just unusually slow starting the generator tonight. Or perhaps the generator had failed. Clifford
Parker must be pounding his fists in anger. He was an en-
gineer and prided himself on the reliability of his ingenious
gadgets. His swimming pool, for example, had a detector that
could discriminate between the falling body of a small child
and the splash of a ball.

And now a gasoline motor, his simplest device, had failed.
As soon as I opened the door, I would hear his angry shouting.

But the latch on the sliding door was jammed. How annoying. None of the gadgets upon which we depended was
working tonight. The lights, the Parkers' generator, and now
my door. At least my flashlight still burned.

I jiggled the latch again. I shook the door, I kicked at it,
put my shoulder to it. It did not move a single inch along
its shiny aluminum track.

It had never jammed before. How odd. I must tell Lucy.
She was a great fixer of household things. She would be able
to fix this . . . what was it now . . . this . . .

How strange. The word slipped my mind.

I knew it just a moment ago. Or was it just a moment ago.
Could it be as long as yesterday?

I couldn't ask her to fix something I could not remember.

How she would laugh at me, oh dear yes, how she . . .

And what was her name? My wife's name. I couldn't remember.

I couldn't remember her name. What was wrong with me?

I was standing in front of a door, trying to open it.

I seemed to be forgetting everything.

The lights had gone out. . . .

I was in Florida. I had come to live in Florida some years ago. With my wife. . . .

Whose name I'd forgotten.

I had come here to live. The lights had gone out. Only my flashlight was still burning.

Logically. Approach the problem logically.

My flashlight was burning. Yet when I shined it through the glass it did not seem to penetrate. The light made little ripples for a few feet, like a stone falling in water; then the dark closed over it.

I was drowsy. Wouldn't she laugh if I were fast asleep in my chair when she came home.

How annoying not to remember her name.

Logically. Try. Again.

My flashlight. It was burning brightly. But there was no reflection from the other side of the glass.

I was pleased with that discovery. Rather scientific of me, even.

So, logically again.

I turned the flashlight full on my face and peered ahead at the glass.

There was no reflection. None at all.

None.

Now I was no longer sure I stood at the window. I was not sure where I was.

I heard one short gasp—I hardly cared. It didn't matter. Nothing did. Because I knew. I knew what I had come here to do.

L U C Y

¶ All through the house I called for him: "Stephen, I'm home." I even looked in his study, though of course he never went there in the evenings anymore.

Finally I found the heap of clothes in the living room. I hadn't realized he was that small.

He had opened the curtains. Imagine. Six months ago he insisted I make curtains for that very window. He always drew them tight at the very first sign of evening and kept them closed until morning.

I thought slowly: *Why are the curtains opened?*

And: *Stephen, stop being so foolish and get up.*

"Oh," I said. Aloud now. "Oh."

I turned Stephen over—he was twisted face down. His arms flopped about, they looked so terrible flung out along the floor that I gathered them back against his sides.

"Stephen, how could you," I told him. "I wasn't even home."

I have never understood how people can confuse sleep and death. Even from a distance you could see that Stephen was dead. The face, the angle of the body, it's nothing like the living. Death looks emptied, hollowed.

Around my ears there was a kind of singing and hissing. I had the ridiculous thought that Stephen's soul had clung to this room, waiting, and was now streaming to freedom past me.

My skin tickled as if something had brushed it lightly, a leaf or a bird's feather.

"Stephen," I said aloud, "did the door have to be opened to let you out?"

He slipped away, saying nothing. After all the years we'd been married. . . .

¶ I tiptoed from the room (whom would I disturb?), closing the door gently. From the bedroom I dialed the emergency number that was stenciled in red on the back of the phone. Stephen himself had put it there: 693–1212. He was so careful to plan for every eventuality. Had he foreseen this one? He often talked about the lines of life forces, believed that the spot where all the lines converged was the place of death. The Valley of Kings, he called it sometimes.

He hadn't talked about that today. He seemed no different. At supper, he wasn't as cheerful as usual; he hadn't eaten, but that meant nothing.

I ought not to have left him.

He had been so annoyed with me that he had gone away when I was out of the house. Deliberately.

Nonsense. Ridiculous.

I waited for the police in the driveway, fifty feet away from the house.

¶ As for the rest, well, I had been through so many funerals during the long years of Stephen's ministry that I felt perfectly at home. I even expected Stephen himself to hurry in at any moment, apologizing for being late.

From being the chief guest at a dinner, he had suddenly become the main course . . . or so Thomas put it.

It was Thomas' habit to rub salt into all wounds, to say the unspeakable.

Paul said nothing. His face showed only terrible fear—real cosmic fear—a child's fear.

I had not thought Paul so devoted to his father.

Edward Henley, Stephen's father, was too frail to travel. He could not come. Instead he sent a film crew.

As with so many things the old man did, the logic was unanswerable. He himself could not be present, he could bury his son only by picture. And that he would do.

Thomas, typically, observed: "So Grandfather is going to use that screening room for something other than porno movies—I shouldn't be surprised if the screen shattered."

Paul said, "It is obscene to show the films of a funeral there."

He was so tight and drawn he seemed like a man becoming violently ill.

"Look, guy," Thomas said to him, "are you all right? I mean, you're not going to pass out or something like that? Do you want a drink? It would steady your nerves."

Paul shook his head firmly.

Thomas turned back to me. "Grandfather introduced Paul and me to the beauties of the female form."

Paul said: "Why are you telling Mother now?"

"Mother doesn't mind and probably she knew anyway. We were like twelve or fourteen, and our eyes practically fell out at the sights on the screen. And didn't he laugh at us."

"Thomas, this isn't the place," Paul said.

"Bless him," Thomas said abruptly. I knew that he spoke of his father now. "I'll miss him."

Looking at the square florid face, I thought: Thomas has buried his father. He has tossed his flower and his handful of dirt; he has lit his candle and he has committed the spirit to everlasting peace. All in those few words. And he is done.

We had the funeral. Stephen's plain gray coffin was lowered by little whining electric motors into the soft Florida ground. I dribbled my handful of earth and dry sand grains blew in the wind. The other mourners left, after the usual handshakes and kisses. My sons and I stood until the grave was completely filled, and smoothed and raked carefully.

I thought about the death cups that you see in country cemeteries, the tiny doll cups left on graves—to comfort the spirits. Often, by the work of wind and rain, the cups stood free of the settling grave, slowly rising on a thin stem of delicately hardened sand.

I wondered if this soil was heavy enough to produce a death cup. I would bring one here and see. It would amuse Stephen to watch it grow. . . .

¶ The movements of mourning were so familiar to me, they lacked all emotional content, all meaning. I knew them so well, I was an actor in a long familiar role.

As if with each of his many funeral services I had buried a bit of Stephen. Like Mithridates and his daily sip of poison, I had immunized myself. When the full dose of grief came, like the poison, I was accustomed to it.

¶ My small house was crowded—Thomas and Claudia, Paul and Jane. (Their children had not come. Paul's were cared for by their regular nurse and Thomas' had been left in their own charge. "Town's pretty safe," Thomas said, "and they're used to taking care of themselves.") We were all excessively polite and thoughtful. We were all drawn thin and weary. Claudia and Jane managed best—they were fond of each other.

Not so my sons. Since their teens they had carefully avoided each other. Thomas' mordant humor annoyed Paul. And the more Paul showed impatience, the more outrageous Thomas became.

Still we managed together for a week after the funeral. Jane, so efficient, became a kind of babysitter for Claudia. They were always together, they did the housework, they saw to the garden and the yard. And each time Claudia left the screen door ajar, Jane closed it without a single word of complaint. Thomas kept me amused. And active. We went for walks on the beach, for walks to town; we went to the college to collect the books and papers Stephen had left there. Thomas was always relaxed, at ease, ready to go anywhere but just as ready to stop when I tired. Paul saw to everything else. The business end of death, you might say.

We were a family unit, each part working smoothly, while I, the matriarch, sat in the position of honor, and reaped the benefits of their labor. . . .

A week after the funeral Mr. Anthony Baldwin arrived.

He was gray haired and smooth faced; he wore a navy tie, and a summer suit that I have always called seersucker though it is undoubtedly some kind of polyester cord. He looked neat and crisp and eminently respectable.

He had been sent by Stephen's father.

"Mr. Henley proposes to establish a trust fund for Mrs. Stephen Henley."

So very long ago, I thought. . . . We'd been married only a few months, I had just begun to suspect my first pregnancy, when Stephen had outlined his father's proposal to me. Life insurance, he'd called it. His life insurance. And now of course, payment was due. . . .

Stephen's father had remembered. Of course he'd remembered. He would honor an arrangement with Stephen, if no one else. . . . I myself had forgotten. I had never thought of Stephen dying. He was younger than I. His ailments were so minor; his diabetes and his emphysema were so well controlled—I had had no suspicion, no intimation of his death.

Paul jumped to his feet and took a few nervous paces across the small living room. "It's a generous and thoughtful offer, Mr. Baldwin. But my brother and I are more than willing and quite able to support our mother."

I blinked a few times, sleepily. . . . Stephen had been so serious when he'd explained it all to me. You must listen very carefully, he said, you must understand. It will be very important when that time comes. . . . And the time was now, it seemed.

Mr. Baldwin was on his feet now, too. Courteously, formally explaining. "Mr. Henley is an aging man, but he is still very much in control of his faculties. He has very precise plans for the disposition of his estate. Most of it, three-quarters to be exact, will go to charity. I needn't bother you with the details, some of his arrangements are as complex as they are precise. The remaining quarter of the estate he bequeathed to his son, Stephen. It is this amount he now proposes to give —without restriction on its use—to his son's widow. He suggests the establishment of a trust as the simplest way to manage such a sum. There is certainly nothing improper in that. And there may even be a decided tax advantage."

Paul said, "My mother cannot accept."

Why were none of them talking to me? Was I not visible to them?

"Paul, you're being a goddamn pompous ass," Thomas said.

"Wait a minute," Paul said, "I resent that."

"Why don't you ask. I bet Mother knows more about this than we do."

"As long as I live, my mother will not need his charity."

"Life insurance," I said. They all jumped. As if there'd been an explosion. "Stephen called it his life insurance when he explained the plan to me years ago."

Thomas chuckled triumphantly. "I thought Pop would have arranged something."

"Mother, please," Paul said, "you're too upset to think about this now."

"Yes," I said, "I am. And that is why your father settled it so long ago."

"It's degrading," Paul said. "Don't take it."

"Take it," Thomas said.

Why were they saying anything? What part did they have in this? Oh Stephen, how very clever you were . . . to understand . . . that bread from our sons would be bitter. . . .

"There's nothing to discuss, really," I said to Mr. Baldwin. "My husband knew of this plan, and he approved of it."

Just then, for the first and only time since Stephen's death, I nearly crumbled, nearly found refuge in hysterics, comfort in tears. Because I thought: *I have reached the security and independence Stephen planned for me. He arranged for me to climb over his dead body into freedom and dignity and peace. . . .*

I noticed that my hands were clenching tightly into fists. *If I don't relax them now,* I thought, *I am lost. Forever. Grief without end. Stephen, come back. . . .*

Using the thumb of my right hand, I began the tedious job of prying my fingers open one by one. When I had done that, I placed my hands, palms down, on my knees.

My voice was steady and my eyes dry. I had come through. Again. If I felt anything at all, I felt only weariness.

"Please go ahead," I said to Mr. Baldwin.

Some hours later, when Mr. Baldwin was finally ready to leave, Thomas and Paul and I walked with him to his car. Paul was furiously angry and obviously sulking. He'd hardly said a word; his thin handsome face was empty of color. Thomas, on the other hand, was in his most expansive mood. He reminded me of nothing so much as a small-town alderman campaigning for re-election.

"I shall be back in touch with you very shortly, Mrs. Henley." Mr. Baldwin unlocked his car door.

Everyone shook hands, formally.

"Have a good flight," Thomas said.

"I can see that my mother looks forward to a comfortable future," Paul said politely.

"Comfortable?" Thomas gave his short rasping laugh and scowled up at the blazing afternoon sky. "You got to be kidding, guy. She'll be a rich old lady, that's what she'll be. She can even buy a new husband."

Paul, with all the strength of his slight body, punched his brother in the face.

That was the first effect of my legacy, a fight between my sons.

Thomas fell backwards across the hood of Mr. Baldwin's car. Clifford Parker, across the street, stopped pruning his hibiscus bushes and straightened up to have a better look. Behind us someone—Claudia or Jane—drew in her breath with a hissing shriek. Thomas, sprawling across the hood of the car, only laughed. "You stupid bastard, oh you stupid bastard." Paul moved toward him again.

Mr. Baldwin began blowing the car horn. A shocking sound, that single electronic note. Paul turned away. Thomas rolled off the hood. Mr. Parker dropped his pruning shears and came trotting to the curb. I put my hands to my ears.

The horn stopped. Mr. Baldwin leaned out the window, his gray hair unruffled, his face implacably polite.

"If you would excuse me, I really must catch my plane."

¶ Paul and Jane moved to a hotel that night. Jane was very annoyed with him. "How silly," she kept saying. "A fight, how ridiculous."

"You know," Thomas said after they had gone, "she's an all-right gal."

Claudia looked at him over the rims of her half glasses. Her thick dark hair, carelessly brushed, had become a bird's nest of curly ends and straggling bits. Her face, with its wide mouth and heavy lower lip, was extraordinarily beautiful. "Thomas," she said lazily, "I do believe you are lusting after your sister-in-law."

"Of course I am, dear lady." He winked at her and then at me. "But fear not. My ambition overreacheth my ability."

Claudia sighed, smiled, and went back to her crossword puzzle.

He fingered the lump over his eye. "Didn't think old Paul had it in him. . . . Mother, you just can't put this house together the way it was when we were children. Look at us—a fistfight not a week after the funeral."

I couldn't put it back together. That was true. My family was gone. My sons were not brothers anymore; they were men who kept an uneasy truce. My husband was dead.

And that was that.

I found myself saying over and over again, in the passing days: *That is that.*

Thomas and Claudia left. I waved them goodbye with a sense of relief. Jane left a few days later—one of the children had come down with flu. Paul stayed, dutifully handling all legal matters. The people at the county courthouse came to know him and to like him. He had the gentle sort of humor that appealed to old people and small-town folk.

But he too had to leave. I took him to the airport and watched the STOL plane lumber down the runway, its long wings flopping at each asphalt joint. After a waddling run it hopped quickly into the air and disappeared in the heat haze.

I drove home, remembering to stop at the grocery for a quart of milk.

The empty house seemed dark, though it was only mid-afternoon. I went to Stephen's study but stopped, my hand on the knob. No. There was nothing for me there.

That is that.

The phone rang. I ignored it. And took a long cool shower. Something I never did in the middle of the afternoon. I changed my clothes too: my familiar faded blue slacks and sleeveless white shirt. I combed my hair and put on lipstick and sprayed a bit of perfume.

The row of perfume bottles on my dresser, the gifts of my sons at Christmas and Easter and birthdays and various anniversaries—Vol de Nuit, L'Heure Bleu, Jicky, Carnet de Bal. Lovely names, provocative names, lovely scents. Applied to sunburned wrinkled old skin.

Anyway, this close to the Gulf, the salt air destroyed all scents. . . .

On the bedside telephone Stephen's carefully printed emergency numbers.

Could I call them to report that I was drowning in silence, smothering in empty air, attacked by emptiness. . . .

I walked through the house, my sneakers silent on the polished floors. In the living room I detected a slight sound, a mouse, perhaps. I followed it. Sherlock Holmes never gave up. Sherlock must trace it to its lair, and there set a trap to smash its neck. . . .

I prowled around and around the room, exaggerating my pursuit, pausing midway in a step, frozen, Indian scout on the prowl, Natty Bumppo to the life. Oh mouse, your days are numbered. . . .

I finally traced the tiny rustling to the electric clock. As I watched the second hand rotate I wondered why I hadn't noticed before. Perhaps there'd been no sound when the clock was new. Perhaps rustling in a clock was synonymous with arthritis in a human.

Or perhaps it only started rustling when Stephen died in this room. The way mirrors are supposed to cloud.

The phone again. I could see it vibrate. Anger? Annoyance? Impatience?

Whatever. I ignored it. I went for a slow walk around the neighborhood. No one was out. The sun was too hot for garden work, the school bus had not yet deposited its children at the edge of their yards, the business day was not yet over.

Quiet empty lines of street. A faint rumble of traffic from the expressway. The slight sad swish of palm fronds. Occasional bird chatter (not much, they too were sheltering from the heat). The street ended at the Gulf and I walked across the swept white sand of the town beach. Mornings and late afternoons these palm-shaded benches, these palm-thatched cabanas would be filled with old people, sitting, or playing checkers, or talking without listening for an answer. I even once saw a chess game. Were they really playing or just pretending?

I will never join this group, I thought, no matter how old I get. I will never sit in the cool, measuring out the breaths of my body in boredom.

Better to be like Stephen's father.

Oh yes, his father. I had a letter from him yesterday, a short, polite, and formal letter. He was delighted I'd accepted the trust fund. Mr. Baldwin would have everything arranged soon. I was also to understand that this was a gift, without conditions, that I had every right to remarry, if I so choose.

The phrase leaped at me, made me slightly nauseated. The old man went on to insist on that point. You have many good years ahead (I snickered silently), you have many qualities calculated to endear you to some good man; you are handsome, you are pleasant, a good organizer, a good housekeeper, and now you have an income. . . .

Trust the old man to drive up my blood pressure.

I walked along the town's sands, rake-patterned, past the town's palms, carefully stripped of all ripening coconuts lest they fall on some ancient head. There was a breeze blowing, as always. The water was choppy, as always. And there on the horizon were the white horses, tossing their manes. That is what Stephen called them, following the ancient Greeks, who had noted that particular wave shape in the Aegean.

So Stephen said.

And so I, an old woman, stood on a sun-baked strip of Florida shore and looked at wind-tossed water through the eyes of long-dead poets.

The manes were flying today. Half-closing my eyes, I saw

the flow of their backs and their muscular withers. I saw the high arch of their necks. They were crowded together, running side by side. Yoked into chariot teams, they seemed forever rounding a corner at top speed. A race. A battle.

Had my eyes only been sharper, I would have seen the whole. Seen winners and losers, the cheering crowd or the massed legions gathered there. . . . Strange illusion that puts the deficiency in the perceiver's mind.

The white manes wheeled in their orderly ranks. Endless parades of racing riders streaming on the waves.

The same wind ticked my hair against my cheeks. My legs ached, I'd stood stock-still too long. I began walking, gritting my teeth as capillaries and heart began the tedious business of forcing blood through my diminishing pathways.

I imagine my vascular structure as a maze of garden walks that are being steadily overgrown; eventually they will not be passable at all. The rampant spread of decay will finally triumph.

Strange sort of fancy, isn't it? But most old people have visions of death. One of Stephen's congregation used to talk about the Man in the Bright Nightgown. He'd say: "The man in the bright nightgown, he's around here a lot, I saw him yesterday. . . ." Afterwards, Stephen explained: "He's obviously put the image of the Angel of Death to his own use. A Death Angel would presumably be black, but he has added the Christian hope of eternity and turned it into a gleaming Angel Gabriel."

I suppose that was exactly what he had done. But in those days we, Stephen and I, were still too young to understand the fantasies of an old mind . . . like my overgrown garden. And, oh yes, Stephen's point of intersecting lines.

He'd talk about it occasionally, though he wasn't really

too clear or definite—which was unusual because he was a
very precise man. Almost, he seemed to be talking to himself.
. . . He saw his life as a series of lines and directions, an
existence charted on graph paper, like a school exercise, vec-
tors arcing across time. Where they intersected, that was
death.

I walked methodically along the streets to my house.

There was a police car at the curb and a very young policeman was emerging from the back yard. "Miss Lucy," he said,
"I am relieved to see you."

I recognized him now. Herbert Addams. He once worked
at the library, a tall gawky thin boy. He still hadn't put on
any weight. . . .

"Hello, Herbert, did you find a burglar in my yard?"

We moved to the shade of the big bougainvillaea trellis.

"We had a call," he said, "that you were not answering
your phone and would we please check."

The purple bougainvillaea flowers were really a very ugly
color, I thought; I must try to start some of the white. "I've
been down at the beach, Herbert, so of course my phone
didn't answer. My family should know better."

He smiled the shy wistful smile of all young men with
heartshaped faces. "I think it was your son."

"It probably was. Herbert, do you know the name of
those bushes? They seem to come up everywhere."

He glanced at the tall bushes with their tiny clumps of
sweet flowers. "Not really," he said. "My mother calls them
wild gardenia."

"Oh? I've been calling them cashmere bouquet because
they *looked* like that should be their name."

His radio squawked. "If you're all right," he said, "I'll be
moving off."

"I'm fine," I said. "My family was very silly."

Inside the phone was ringing again. I smiled at it very politely and did not answer. It would be one of my sons or their wives. Or even one of their children. They had lately taken up the nauseating habit of having the children telephone Grandma.

I didn't want to talk to any of them.

Not now. Perhaps not ever. I immediately corrected myself. I would of course. And soon. Because they were my sons.

Now there were too many images of them jumbled in my memory. Paul's fist making that dull thud into Thomas' forehead. Thomas' raucous laugh. As a baby he laughed in his sleep, a deep satisfied chuckle that was, from a child in diapers, annoying in its superiority. . . . It often woke me at night, that old man's chuckle in a baby's body.

And Paul, so silent, so invisible. He hardly cried; he was never the least demanding. Handsome, and blond, and somehow transparent. When he was a child, he had the habit of playing silently by himself (sometimes he'd just lie flat on his back and stare at the ceiling) in an empty room. I often stepped on him—I have a habit of entering rooms quickly —and once I stumbled and spilled hot coffee all over him. . . .

The telephone was still ringing. Would they never give up!

Patience. My sons were showing their love for me. I must remember that. However annoying, it was evidence of love.

I could see them all so clearly. Thomas and Paul. And Jane, so small and pretty—in her mid-thirties she still seemed a model from *Mademoiselle*. And Claudia, careless and sulky and peevish. . . . These two repositories of my sons' seed, nurturers of my continuing line. . . .

Dear Lord, I was being foolish.

I answered the phone. "Yes!" I said, and listened for ten minutes while Thomas told me how worried they had been. Love between the generations was a burdensome chore.

¶ My days passed slowly, calmly. Each distinguished by some small happening. Tuesday I planted a rosebush called Brownell that is supposed to withstand our heat and sun. (Here most roses bloom themselves to death in two years.) On Wednesday I scraped and cleaned the rusting barbecue grill. Thursday I waxed the car. Evenings were marked the same way: the evening I watched *The Merchant of Venice* on television, the evening I presided at the Board of Education meeting, the evening I went out for dinner—whose house didn't matter. I myself could not remember a day later.

And through it all, I felt no grief. Only a sense of emptiness, of finality.

And that is that.

I sat up late at night, thinking, trying to understand. Sat up so late that Herbert Addams, on night duty now, came tapping on the window to be sure I was still all right.

Something lacking in me. How could I let Stephen go without even a parting wave of grief?

I had grieved for Harold Evans, my first husband. Why not now?

The more I questioned, the less clear the answers became.

I even began thinking about Harold Evans again. Imagine. I hadn't thought of him for decades. Now he was back. And old memories danced about my mind. I was eighteen, on a miserable Greek freighter, rolling and wallowing in the Aegean, rusting plates clanking and sprinkling flakes of paint into the water. The passengers—mostly Turks—were violently seasick. Below decks reeked with vomit. My cabin, which I shared with a German missionary nurse, was clean enough—she was careful to keep it so—but her muffled retchings never seemed to stop. I entered the cabin only to sleep. All the rest of the time I spent on deck. I only needed to be careful where I stepped, to be sure my scarf did not trail into a frothy puddle, to brace myself on the rolling deck without touching anything. The second evening Harold Evans stood beside me at the rail. He lit a cigarette and the flame flashed across his thin face. "Are you managing to survive?"

He was dark and slender and short. He could have been a Turk or a Greek. I had not noticed him in the crowd of passengers when we boarded. I had noticed only the north Europeans—the German nurse, a couple of Swiss botanists, on holiday like me, a white-haired lady from Yorkshire who had something to do with Methodist missions. Harold Evans had simply been part of the crowd.

"I'm doing very well," I said, "though it can't be because I'm used to the ocean. I live in BEA." (Everybody called it that. Properly it was British East Africa. Now of course it's Kenya.)

"I've never been there," he said.

"I was born in a place called Harold's Hotel," I said, because I had always found the name of that tiny dusty fly-bedeviled town amusing.

"My name is Harold," he said. "Any significance to that?"

He was an archaeologist. Currently he was interested in an ancient trading city called Cyzicus or Bandirma. The town's badge was a tuna fish, he said.

We were young and on a strange ocean. His American

accent was very attractive as we stood talking and balancing on the shifting deck. "The water isn't really rough," he said, "but it is a particularly nasty chop. You can see why the ancient sailors stayed coastwise along this stretch. And how did you get out in this part of the world?"

Accident, I told him. By accident. I had been on a tour of the Holy Land with my grandfather, a quiet man deeply devoted to his harsh Calvinist faith. The tour was such a success—he drew such spiritual comfort from the stones of Jerusalem, the rubble of Jericho—that he extended our trip to include Rome. He felt the need, he said, to see the city of anti-Christ. Predictably, he was horrified. His evening prayers grew longer and louder as if he would shake the walls of the Vatican. Within a week he was ready to go home—his plantation adjoined my parents' land. But the voyage to Mombasa was very long and tiresome—we stopped at Cyprus. He found life so pleasant there that he decided to stay a few weeks. He also decided that I should have a holiday myself, and see the Greek islands.

"Cyprus is a great deal more pleasant than this bit of water." Harold Evans laughed. "You made a bad deal."

"I don't think so," I said huffily. "I've had a lovely trip and I'll be very sorry when it's time to go home."

"Home?" He turned the word around on his tongue as if it tasted bad. "Do you miss it?"

"Sometimes." I missed the dazzling African light that varnished everything it touched, giving even grass huts the illusion of substance and dignity. The deceptive light that shortened distances into fractions of actual fact.

"Did you miss it when you were in England last year?"

"How on earth did you know I'd been in England?"

"Your Fraulein told me before she disappeared. By the way, did she go overboard?"

"She's in her bunk, quite safe."

"And the Captain told me. And the last customs inspector. They'd seen your papers, you know."

"But why would you bother?"

"I was interested."

He lit another cigarette, cupping his hands against the wind. He had a thin face, a beaked nose, and now there was spray in his eyebrows and his hair. But, I learned, even on the quietest day, miles from the ocean, Harold Evans carried that same windblown look with him.

❡ He reminded me of a man I'd seen the year before in Hyde Park. I was spending a few months in London with my Aunt Rebecca—my parents had insisted on the visit. Was it some vague idea of the Season? They had neither the money nor the connections to make that possible. Was it some yearning for a world they'd left? An attempt to give at least one of their children a taste of European life? My brothers—they were twins—clearly reflected our mother's Boer ancestry. They were short, thickset, incredibly powerful. As boys they wrestled wild calfs for sport. As men they worked with our father on the coffee plantation, and were not the least interested in what lay beyond the clear hard skies of their particular bit of Africa. (One was murdered by the Mau Mau, the other emigrated to Australia. I heard from him only once. The hunting, he said, was simply frightful.)

Anyway, despite the poor state of the coffee economy, I went to England. And I went to Hyde Park very early one misty morning. My cousin, whom I disliked in a mild but definite way, explained: "He always comes this way. He's Cunningham-Graham. You know, the writer." Well, I didn't know. And I thought it profoundly stupid to be lurking along bridle paths for a glimpse of a man I was never going to meet. My Aunt Rebecca, however, declared this one of the great sights of the country, ranking with Canterbury or Stonehenge or Stratford. (My aunt was happiest arranging things. She should have been a tour director.)

"There," my cousin said in a hushed voice. "There."

He came cantering out of the fog, passing quite close to us. The first thing I noticed was his boots. I had read about people seeing themselves in bootpolish and I'd always thought it a figure of speech. No more—his boots were absolutely mirror-like. Then I noticed the way he sat that horse, a big gray. He might have been a centaur out for a morning adventure, he was so much one body, one being with that animal. I caught my breath sharply and my cousin nodded approvingly. Oh damn her, I thought. . . . He was a small man, very slight, with a thin hawk face and hair that swept straight back from his face, over his ears, as if a gale were blowing through it. He was only cantering sedately through the wet green of a London morning, but with him he carried a sense of urgency and natural violence, of storms and mad dashes to safety. . . .

Harold Evans possessed that same tension. That feeling of drama and adventure. Of danger and crisis.

I told him of his resemblance to Cunningham-Graham— he smiled and shrugged. "At least I'm in good company."

He talked rapidly and constantly. At first I had trouble with his American accent, but then quite suddenly I found that he had no accent at all.

He spent hours explaining to me the precise problems of ancient trading ships along this coast. "Trade routes are the keys to understanding ancient civilizations," he insisted. "Culture follows trade, not the other way around.

"I'm still a college student," he added abruptly.

"A little old for that, aren't you?"

"How English that remark is. . . . You see, I quit college to go into business with my father for five years. We make hideous furniture that people buy because they think it is exquisitely beautiful. Then I spent two years in Turkey and two more in Italy, mostly Sardinia. Fantastic ruins there, and the stupid Italians don't know enough to protect what they've got. You should see what I was able to take out quite legally. . . . Anyway, this fall I go back to Princeton."

For the rest of the trip—three days—I listened to him talk about his plans, his interests, his fascination with archaeology. I don't think I said more than two dozen words—and when we parted, I certainly never expected to see him again. He was going to Turkey, I knew, to finish some work. He did not say "I'll write," did not ask for my address.

I was vaguely depressed and restless when I joined my grandfather. I found myself missing Harold Evans' constant chatter. I dismissed all such thoughts and concentrated on the details of traveling: the long shipboard days to Mombasa, the endless trip by rail, the dusty lurching hours in a cart behind small bony African oxen. Then we were home.

My parents and my brothers waited on the veranda—I'd sent a syce some hours before to announce our arrival. I had a half-sad, half-pleasant stirring of stomach emotions when I saw the sprawling grass-roofed house where I'd lived almost all my life. When I was a child the house had a mud floor, plain hard-packed mud, and all night long little insects rustled and crackled and squeaked through the walls. It was much nicer now, with floors and proper English furniture. The dusty yard was filled with my mother's special flowers, and everything was varnished by that incredible African light. Everything. The hill slopes. The flowering trees. The shambas. The Kikuyu. The rondavels. The towering termite castles. As a child I'd been terrified by the stories of gigantic queen termites buried deep in each castle, bloated insects producing egg after egg, by the millions, year after year. Stories to frighten children with.

Two hours home and I found myself wondering if I'd ever been away. Time had no real meaning in Africa, there were no marks of the past: no graveyards, no temples, not even a recently abandoned farmhouse. The shambas vanished quickly and completely. People had lived here for thousands of years without leaving a mark on their earth.

Everything was transient; everything was timeless too.

My twin brothers grinned their hellos and then forgot about me, my father kissed me and went back to work. My mother was delighted. "There's been nobody to talk to," she explained. Which was not true. My mother talked steadily all day long, to the cook whose name was Abdul and who was the ugliest Swahili I have ever seen, to her chickens and ducks and assorted small animals, to her flowers, to the young coffee trees in their special nursery down by the river bank. "You are the only person it's worth talking to," my mother corrected herself.

Life settled into its predictable pattern of disasters. A freak rainstorm damaged some of the young coffee plants. Battler ants marched through one corner of the kitchen, nearly chewing off our old dog's leg. My mother's pet duikers escaped and she fretted for their safety. Something got into the henhouse and devastated the flock. . . . My mother's flock was never very large because it was decimated so often. She always rebuilt it in the same ill-protected building.

This was the life I had always known. My father and my brothers seemed a bit noisier now as they shouted and cursed and argued with each other and with the vague inefficient Kikuyu. Predictably, every evening the walls shook with fist-thumping arguments. Yet the twins—Peter and Cyril—had great respect and love for our father. When he died some years later of a blackwater fever, his sons grieved more than his wife. (She had learned a harsh fatalism in Africa, something close to the natives' impassivity in suffering.) Cyril took to his bed for a week, not eating, rarely drinking, rigid with grief. Peter loaded three of his guns and set out to kill everything in sight. He shot at birds and animals and insects; he undoubtedly would have fired on people too, but word had gone round and everyone kept well out of range. He stayed out for days; he walked all the way over to the railway bridge at Marshalltown and shot at the train there. Luckily he misjudged the distance across that shimmering brown plain. Finally, my mother brought him home.

But that was the future. The present was my mother's struggles to upgrade her hens. She'd been at this for years and she was a constant failure. She successfully bred for hardiness, but in doing so she produced a strong trait of sterility. After a couple of generations, her great experiments came to a natural halt.

"You have to introduce another strain, Mother."

"Not so easy," she said triumphantly. "Most breeds won't stand the African weather."

"Then we'll just have the same scrubby chickens we've always had."

Her eyes glittered. "It's a challenge," she said firmly.

Life to my mother was a series of challenges.

(But only so long as my father was alive. After his death, she found the world too full of problems. She left Africa, stopping first in the Anglican churchyard to say goodbye to her husband, and went off to London. She lived into her mid-eighties, in discreet peace, with her sister Rebecca.)

¶ My father bought a new truck. It was a major expense, that truck, and it required constant attention. Still, he enjoyed tinkering with it, and when the roads were dry the truck was certainly a lot more convenient than any bicycle or horse or oxcart.

(I can still see those small scrawny African oxen, covered with flies, too apathetic to twitch their tails, plodding along resentfully, dragging carts piled so high that it seemed they could not move them at all.)

One afternoon my father was working on the truck, he had both sides of the hood propped open, and as he tinkered he whistled shrilly. My father, who was quite tone deaf, only whistled when he was particularly happy.

My brothers were out, my mother was lying down in the dark rustly interior of the house, I was sitting on a corner of the veranda doing the accounts. (My mother refused to touch the books, and my father did them badly. I rather enjoyed them, with their neat precise judgments of profit and loss.) . . .

When Harold Evans rode up our dusty rutted road on a bicycle.

He came straight up to the veranda, leaned his bike against the house, flattening most of my mother's cosmos.

His face was streaked yellow and brown and even red—all the colors of the clay he had ridden through. (Red, I found myself thinking, where was there a band of red clay. . . .) His light eyes were startling in his darkened face. They had something of the opaque look of blind men's eyes.

I sat perfectly still, the account books spread out over the small table in front of me. I stared. I wasn't thinking anything, I was simply—and emptily—surprised.

He put one foot on the step, leaned his elbow on his knee and smiled at me. "You look just exactly the way I thought you would."

"I do?"

He laughed. "I borrowed the constable's bike—nice of him, wasn't it? Told him I had to see a girl and he practically insisted I take it."

"I am glad to see you." Shocked surprise was fading to pleasure.

He laughed again. His teeth were square and quite short. They appeared under his lips like small peeping objects.

"It would be dreadful to bike all that way in the heat only to find you weren't talking to me."

"Oh," I said, "oh yes." I didn't understand him, but I didn't bother. I was enjoying the prickling feeling of unexpected happiness: He had come to see me. To see me. Me.

"Yes," he repeated, "it was quite a ride. . . . Where's your father?"

"Fixing his truck. Why?"

"Best see him first. You know, tell the master when you set foot on his territory." A hazy blue eye winked at me. "Where's the truck?"

"It's down there, past the kitchen. Just across from that rondavel, see it?"

He nodded. "Now, off to see the paterfamilias."

Automatically I moved to go with him. He stopped me with a grimy hand on my arm. His touch was so hot and dry I wondered if he had fever. "I'd prefer you to stay here," he said flatly.

The change in tone startled me. I stood stock-still and watched him walk rapidly along the path. In mid-step he pulled the bicycle clips from his ankles and stuffed them into his hip pocket. His shirt was stained with sweat and plastered tight across his shoulders. The back of his neck was deeply tanned, not the tan of African sun through the thin air of these uplands, but the deep mahogany tan of saltwater.

"Lucy," my mother called, "did I hear voices?" She sounded breathless and a little muffled. She always removed her corsets for her nap and she must be struggling back into them now. She did them lying flat in bed, bouncing and tugging at the laces.

Harold Evans was out of sight beyond the thorn corral. I hesitated a moment more, then followed.

My father was leaning against the truck's fender, holding one hand to his back and stretching carefully, as if he had just straightened up.

They were past the first words of introduction. My father, who always liked new people, was beginning to break into his wide friendly grin.

"I've come here to ask for your daughter," Harold Evans said.

My father's half-formed grin faded. "You what?"

"I want to marry your daughter."

I blinked at the sweat-stained back. And echoed my father silently: You what?

My father wiped his forehead with the back of a dirty

hand and sat down heavily on a low wooden stool. It had been made by my brothers when they were very small and the legs were uneven. My father had to lean slightly to the left to correct its lurch.

"Would you say that again?"

Harold Evans shrugged. I could see his shoulders go up and down. "I simply wanted you to know why I am here."

"Oh," my father said, "oh."

"After all, it isn't as if I lived in the next county. It's much more difficult. I'm an American, and I have to go back soon. I want Lucy to come with me, so we must be married here."

My father had both hands on his knees and was staring at him silently.

Harold went on: "I'm quite prepared to outline the details of my financial situation. Or answer any questions. I'm sure you'll have some. I may have just dropped from the blue, you know, but I want to be fair and direct and have everything above board. I really don't want you thinking there is anything strange about this."

"I don't know whether there is anything strange," my father said, "but you'll admit that it is unusual."

Me. I thought suddenly. They are talking about me.

Harold Evans said: "When I met Lucy on shipboard, I knew I wanted to marry her. I let a month pass and waited to be sure. I am sure."

My father hadn't moved. "You met on a ship?"

"A miserable Greek ship. I think we were the only two passengers who weren't seasick."

"That would be the start of a friendship," my father said. I couldn't tell if he was joking. It was the sort of thing he might say in all seriousness.

"I've brought my last bank statement—I've been away

from home so long I use Lloyd's. I've also brought the last few
letters from my parents; it might give you some insight into
the kind of people they are. There's my passport of course.
And I remembered that my older brother has done some business with a bank in Johannesburg, so I cabled them for
family references."

"A great many cables." My father was thinking of their
cost. His thrifty soul was startled.

"I should have even more replies quite soon," Harold
Evans went on. "The dean of Christ Church at home. I was
baptized there, but now only my parents are members." He
sounded almost apologetic. "And the American consul at
Naples is a great friend of mine; I'm sure I'll hear from him.
We worked together on the Sardinian ruins. . . . But I
think probably the cables are simply accumulating in Nairobi.
I shall have to see about them."

"Well," my father said, "well, well."

He was impressed. Or perhaps he was just irritated.

"It seems silly to you?" Harold Evans put one foot on the
truck's runningboard. "I suppose it must. But it would have
been utterly foolish of me to arrive here knowing nobody
and with *no* sort of introduction."

"These days I thought young people arranged everything
and set the date and only told you about it when their plans
were complete."

Harold Evans said: "Lucy and I have not made detailed
plans because I have not formally asked her to marry me."

"I wondered why she hadn't said anything." My father
got up very slowly from his unsteady bench. "How do you
know she will marry you, if you haven't asked her?"

"Oh she will," Harold Evans said, "that's not the problem
at all."

My father rubbed both his hands across his cheeks, leaving long smears of grease. "You might start by asking her."

"Of course," he said. "She's at the house. I told her to wait for me there."

"Well, she didn't," my father said. "She's standing on the path behind you, and she's been there the whole time."

My father pointed straight to me. Before Harold Evans could turn, I raced back to the house, burning with embarrassment. I almost collided with my mother in the main door. She had her stays on now, and her welcoming smile, and she was tucking up the bun of her hair with one hand.

¶ We were married two weeks later. All our neighbors and relatives came for the ceremony. They crowded the veranda and cheered loudly at the end of the service. A few Kikuyus looked on from the edge of the yard—they seemed vaguely puzzled by the unusual festival. My father's truck had been specially cleaned and polished and decorated with bunches of my mother's flowers. Some hours later, after many toasts and a great deal of hugging and kissing, Abdul drove us to town, to the railroad line. I don't think anyone noticed our going. They were all dancing enthusiastically while an accordion thumped out an old Boer tune. Dust spurted like smoke under their prancing feet. From a distance it looked as if they were stamping out fires.

We were married for two years. I grew used to thinking of myself as Mrs. Harold Evans.

¶ We went directly to Princeton, where we rented a small half-house and furnished it hastily. "Terrible junk," Harold said. "No matter. I have to get to work; I can't be bothered."

"Terrible junk," his family said when they came. And they all did—his mother, his father, his four brothers, and that dean from Christ Church who had cabled a character recommendation. (He was an amiable man named Palmerston who had a consuming interest in religious water colors, especially scenes of the crucifixion.) The Evans family was not in the least like Harold. They were all tall, and they were all heavy. Mr. Evans weighed at least two hundred and fifty pounds. He had thinning red hair and a wide face pinched across by a narrow strip of silver-rimmed glasses. He'd not changed those frames for years. They cut deeply into the skin at his temples, dug holes behind his ears, and almost disappeared into his obligingly soft flesh. His wife was blond, almost as tall, and almost as heavy. The four sons looked exactly like them. Only slight dark Harold Evans was different.

They were pleasant people, very kind in a casual way. But there was something myopic in their gracious generous glance. Something impersonal. I am sure they were kind to their animals in exactly this fashion. It was not that they liked animals so much. Or people so little. But that they simply couldn't see the difference between them.

Their wedding present to us was a car, a black Packard sedan. I gasped when I saw it. I knew little of American cars, but I could see the luxury in every line. Harold did not seem impressed. "Thank God they were practical," he said. "They could have insisted on giving us a houseful of that awful furniture we manufacture, or they could have decided we needed some art. You haven't seen the bronzes in my mother's garden—you wouldn't believe them."

"Harold," I said, "I can't drive."

"No? I'll find somebody to teach you."

He did and I learned quickly. I have always liked machinery and the comforting purr of well-tuned motors.

The car became my only companion. Harold wanted no friends.

"I have no time," he said. "I must finish. People will come later. Now we have only each other. A couple in love needs no one else."

That was of course not quite true.

He went to classes, he knew people by sight, he exchanged casual comments with them. He had conferences with his professors. He had a busy world.

I was almost completely isolated. There were few married students in those days. They were scattered about town and I didn't know them. I might talk briefly with the grocer and nod to the butcher. But that was all. Once or twice I went to the university library, but Harold did not approve of my being on campus. Finally I settled on the public library. Each week I carried off armloads of books, any books. I pulled them from the shelves because their color caught my eye, or their design pleased me. I did not even bother to open their covers until I got home.

I could not endure such aimlessness. I finally planned a course of study—American history. While Harold traced his ancient trade routes around the Mediterranean, I would trace the history of my new country.

I progressed from general textbooks to specialized studies, to biographies of generals and presidents and men of power and influence. After that I moved to the abstract analyses: the economics of the Andrew Jackson era, the corporate structure of western railroads after the Civil War, the theological basis of American government.

I was isolated, true, but not lonely. I'd been raised to be self-dependent. During the rainy season our plantation went months without a single visitor.

What I was not used to was Harold Evans. I saw him, literally, only in bed at night, and all day Sunday when we sat in our separate chairs, reading.

We must have seemed a perfect couple, perfectly adapted to each other. And in a way we were.

In bed in the dark—he always insisted on the dark—his whole frame seemed to grow, as if he were some sort of balloon of flesh and blood. He was devious, he was cunning, he was knowledgeable in ways I hadn't known existed. (My sex education had come from the cattleyard.) He was like a drug, and I was addicted. Evenings after dinner I found myself watching the clock, waiting for bedtime (always ten-thirty). I couldn't concentrate on my book. The fingers of my left hand began to tremble slightly, as I longed for the whirling shuddering dark lit by spasms of pain and glory.

I did not want to need anybody that much. I began to find sex vaguely distasteful, then repellent. My body still cringed in want but my mind had moved away in disgust.

I spent hours in the car, running imaginary errands. Every morning as I swung open the garage doors, I felt a surge of pleasure, of relief. When I was alone driving slowly down some street whose name I didn't know, I was free.

Even Harold noticed the change in my habits. "Wonderful," he said, "that you get such pleasure from driving. I've always hated it myself. Why don't we let you do it all now?"

Why should his words destroy my pleasure? Why should it matter to me that he thought driving a chore, not a skill to display triumphantly. Why should he have such power over my emotions?

"Why," I asked, all my annoyance showing like quills on a porcupine, "do you always denigrate the thing I do?"

He looked at me in blank surprise. "I said I had never liked to drive and that I was delighted you did."

"That's exactly what I mean."

"I drive only because I must," he said, still thinking carefully. "Many people find it exciting but I'm not one of them."

"You didn't think that until I learned to drive."

"I thought it, yes, but I didn't have any choice. Before you learned to drive."

"That isn't the way you made it sound." I was sulking now. And so annoyed with myself I could have screamed. Mistake, I thought, mistake, mistake.

"I would not downgrade your achievement," he said formally. "I assumed you'd know that. And I apologize."

"That's not it," I mumbled.

He continued. "I really ought to have realized that it would embarrass you to drive with me in the car. Yes, I can see that now. In our society the man drives, not the woman. How foolish of me not to have thought of it."

"Yes," I said wearily. Even my anger had gone. He had misunderstood. It wasn't that way, it wasn't that way at all.

I went back to the car and the roads.

I no longer shopped in the neighborhood—too easy, too quick. My bakery was on the Trenton Road. My butcher was in the direction of Philadelphia. And there was the bootlegger, who might be anywhere—he never delivered to the same place twice. The first time I picked up our liquor, I drove to a stationery store on the Bardstown Road, parked outside, leaving the trunk unlocked. I bought two sketching pads and a supply of charcoal. It took no more than five minutes but when I put my package in the trunk, I saw that the bottles were there. All the drive back my hands sweated nervously, I kept imagining a car filled with G-men overtaking me. At home Harold was bent over a set of architectural drawings on the dining table. He had removed the shades from the overhead lights and worked in a blazing glare.

Blinking in the dazzle, he looked at me. "Are you sick? You look so strange. . . ."

I managed a laugh. "I've never broken a law before and I was nervous, that's all."

"Everybody has a bootlegger, you know."

"It's just the first time." I put the four bottles of Scotch in the kitchen cupboard. "I'll be more relaxed when I get used to it."

He nodded, smiled briefly, and went back to his work.

He seemed mildly pleased.

And I did make frequent trips to the bootlegger. Harold liked whiskey. The bottle and the soda syphon always stood ready on the sideboard. We had Scotch before dinner and Scotch during dinner. We never had wine, nor water. (I'd been surprised at first. At my parents' house liquor was very scarce, except for homemade beer, and reserved strictly for holidays and parties.) "Beef and Scotch go well together," Harold would say. "Scotch and anything goes well together."

Whiskey, like sex, relaxed him, expanded him. Each evening he grew larger, each morning he shrank back to his real physical size.

My desire for him increased. Once, driving on the Trenton Road, the full force of my need struck me. It was a physical thing, a jolt, a blow. I pulled the car to a stop, and checked the road behind me—I actually thought I had run over something. When I finally understood, I was so angry I had trouble starting the car again. The gears stuck and grated. I sweated and fought with them. I pushed in the clutch, released it, hunted for the gears, found reverse, shot backwards, stopped so sharply that my neck popped. When I finally did get the right gear, I was crying furious tears.

I had to do something.

I was dependent on a man simply because he was a man; I was trapped by my skin. But I was not limited.

Certainly no one man was so different from another. Dependence on many was better than dependence on one.

And how did one go about finding a lover? Was he browsing in the stacks of the library? Did he stroll by the picket fence of our front yard? Was he hidden by the lilac bushes at the corner? Was he lurking somewhere among the campus buildings in that crowd of faceless men? Was this a game of hide-and-seek where discovery came suddenly?

I was calm now. I no longer had trouble with the car and the driving. I could go on to keep the appointment with Harold's bootlegger, this time a gas station. I had never been there before, knew no one; they would recognize my car's license. I opened the trunk (I had finally learned not to call it the boot, I was becoming Americanized), a young man casually put a package inside, and moved off to check the air pressure in the tires. I closed the trunk and locked it. Then, waiting, I looked around. The short heavy man at the pump, the young boy bending over the tires, his neck blazing with acne. They were greasy and sweaty and dirty. Strange I should notice that. In Africa the supremely strong smells had never bothered me at all. These men ignored me, they went their way without a glance, I might have been another gas pump standing there. I watched the amber fluid sink in the glass tank, paid for it, and drove off. Home.

As I unloaded the things I had bought—a loaf of Russian

black bread, the illegal liquor, a quantity of pale green wool for a scarf I was crocheting—they were called fascinators in those days—I began to see how funny it all was.

I put the things away carefully, and then I sat in one of the two wooden chairs and laid my head on the chilly white porcelain top of the kitchen table.

There wasn't going to be any glamor. My life was going to run its smooth organized way. I may have seen Cunningham-Graham ride by in the early mist, but I'd been standing cold and wet on the grass. And he hadn't noticed me either.

I'd always been standing on the grass—in a sense. I'd even met Harold on a vomit-tinged ship. That was the smell of life, not L'Heure Bleu or any of the other new perfumes that were beginning to appear in the stores.

At least for me. I would make my green wool fascinator and I would be very glad to have it when the winter blew cold and wet. It would keep my hair in order. In a proper sort of way.

And I would owe my virtue to circumstances.

¶ Harold decided not to join that summer's expedition to the ruins in Sardinia.

"I thought that was just exactly what you wanted to do."

"It is," he said, "but the time is wrong. My notes will keep me busy for months."

He showed me the finished chapters—there were three or four—of his study of the ancient trade routes of the Mediterranean. "It's going very well. The press here has already said they'd be interested. . . ."

He was so pleased, so proud. And so was I.

"But wait, Lucia." That was a conceit of his. He refused to

call me by my baptismal name, preferring the Italian Lucia. I thought it rather nice. "Are you getting homesick, or lonesome? Would you like to invite your parents to visit us this summer?"

I could not see my father making the Atlantic crossing after the long slow trip from Africa to England.

"Harold," I said, "perhaps I could meet them in London. If you don't mind."

"Mind? Of course I don't mind, I think it's wonderful." He went back to the business of sorting through his notes, which were arranged neatly in file boxes. And the number of boxes kept growing.

That summer I met my mother in London. At the last minute my father refused to come—he always found an excuse to stay with that expanse of African bush he was slowly turning into a profitable coffee plantation. My mother, her sister Rebecca, and I had a wonderful month. (The cousins I remembered with such dislike had all married and moved away to places like Canada and New Zealand.) My mother asked me to stay longer. My Aunt Rebecca asked me to stay longer. Because I had no idea when I would ever see them again, I stayed.

Harold wrote me twice a week, long chatty pages. He'd adopted a family of stray kittens, he said, and our landlady was furious. He kept them on our back porch for safety. The summer was unusually warm, even for Princeton. That probably meant a cold winter. He had lost or misplaced his flame briar, his favorite pipe; could I find him another? He would try to remember the shop where he'd originally bought it. And did I know what a flame briar was?

I didn't then, but I learned. And when I returned, I brought one with me. Even better—and most extravagant

—I'd gotten a straight briar for him, a magnificent pipe. I'd
also brought back something else, an idea my mother had
given me. When I'd described for her Harold's work on the
ancient trade routes, she immediately said, "Lucy, you must
write children's history books."

Things were so simple to my mother. "History books?"

"Yes." She had a flushed wide-eyed look whenever she was
in pursuit of a plan. "You write an English history for American children, all the kings and wars. You know a lot of history; it was always your best subject in school."

The trip back to New York was rough, the ship slowed to
half-speed, rose and shuddered and fell with each wave. Eventually even that slow progress stopped. We hove to and
waited, thumping and banging in the cold gray foaming seas.

I lay in bed and read—chairs were too uncomfortable—
and waited for mealtimes. There were only about two dozen
of us survivors of seasickness. We all sat at two large tables.
The kitchen stopped serving soup and the waiters handled
coffee and tea as if they were bombs about to explode. "Too
bloody difficult to move about," one old gentleman explained
to me after lunch. "Stay here and wait for tea." He was a perfect John Bull—hard to believe he was real—huffing and
blowing like a stranded whale. "How are you at cards?"

"Not very good," I said.

He huffed again. "Watch us then," he ordered.

Now, my patience for cards had always been limited, and
I wasn't about to spend hours watching other people. "Thank
you," I said, "but I'm going back to my cabin."

"Not sick?" He tilted back his head and peered at me
carefully. "Not sick?"

I felt curiously affronted at the suggestion that my

stomach was weakening. "Oh not at all. I've just got some work to do."

"Work?" He did not believe a word.

"Yes," I said. "I'm writing a book."

I left with as much dignity as I could manage.

It took the best part of an hour to find any suitable paper. The purser finally supplied some long yellow sheets. And, propped on my bed, braced with pillows against the heaving sea, I began a history of England for American children.

My hand ached. I had trouble remembering many details, but when I went through customs in New York, I clutched a bundle of pages. I had reached the time of the first Queen Elizabeth.

Harold met me. He was much thinner—I felt a sudden twinge of guilt for staying away so long—but his welcoming hug was firm and the comforting smell of his pipe tobacco hadn't changed.

At home a line of black and white cats sat on our small porch.

"See how they grew." Harold pointed to them.

"I didn't know there were so many."

"Cats have large families." He grinned. "The old woman almost evicted us because of those animals—I feed them after dark and I keep moving the plates around so she's not likely to catch them."

It was so unlike him—I giggled. "I didn't know you liked cats."

"As a matter of fact"—he stopped in the midst of unlocking the door to think about it—"as a matter of fact, I don't like cats. I loathe cats. I have no idea why I kept them."

The house was neat and very clean. Only the index cards

now lined every available surface. In the twelve weeks I had been gone they'd multiplied immensely.

The dining table was completely covered, and the top of the small buffet. So was the living-room coffee table and the end tables and a new card table set up in the middle of the floor. Only the bed and my dressing table were clear.

"It isn't only cats who have large families," Harold said with a wave. "I've given birth since you've been gone."

I looked around slowly. "You didn't do anything else."

He shook his head. His eyes were glittering and bloodshot, and he rubbed at them occasionally. "Twelve weeks without you," he said, "may be good for working, but it's not good for much else." And he kissed me very gently on the lips.

Away from him I had not felt the slightest flicker of desire. In three months the thought had not crossed my mind.

But now I felt the familiar twitch, the familiar burning, the warm flood that rose from groin to brain until nothing else remained.

Oh no, I thought, oh God no.

The warmth rose steadily, surf pounding.

I don't like this, I thought, I don't like having feelings I can't control. I don't like this at all.

My chest was contracting. It was difficult to breathe. I was drowning.

What happens to me? Why do I die every time, and who is the other person, the one who is left when I have drowned here?

Oh God, I don't *want* anything at all like this.

A funny sort of drowning. In the inevitable resurrection, when the creeping tide had atomized into thin air, I would become myself again. Satisfied, resentful. . . .

Harold said: "There's no food in the house. We'll have to go out."

"Harold," I said, "did you eat at all when I was gone? I mean really?"

"No," he said. "I was busy. Anyway, we all eat too much."

That was the first change. He no longer ate regularly. He preferred snacks at odd times—soup, eaten unheated and undiluted from the can; an apple; a can of salmon. Some days he went completely without solid food. He drank a bit of coffee and a bit of tea and no whiskey at all. The bottle of Scotch stood on a closet shelf.

What happened while I was gone?

"I simplified my life," he said.

Because he seemed healthy and full of energy, and because people finishing scholarly projects were notoriously full of idiosyncrasies—I did not worry. The lines of note cards stayed on the dining table. We (often I alone) had our meals perched at the tile counter in the kitchen, overlooking our small garden. Soon the cats discovered us. They clustered in the yard below, the bolder ones leapt to the windowsill and crouched there, staring at us, pressing so hard against the screen that the tips of their fur passed through the wire.

In the shortening fall days I sat in the garden, writing my children's history. The cats kept me company.

"You don't go driving anymore," Harold said, "do you?"

He was home most days now. He had finished his classes, he would graduate with the next commencement in June. In the meantime he must finish his study of the trade routes, he must do it before beginning graduate school.

That was why I sat in the chilly gray garden. I did not want to be in his way.

When the days became too cold and I had to move inside, I selected a corner of the living room. I'd noticed that he seemed to prefer working in the dining room.

"Do you like to drive anymore?" Harold asked.

"Oh I still like to," I said. "And I still do."

He cleared his throat and watched me a moment. "What are you writing?"

I explained to him.

"Oh," he said, "a fine idea."

Later, when I asked him to find a typist, he said, "You're finished so soon? You can take the manuscript to my typist."

His typist. That must mean progress for him too.

"Harold," I said, "are you almost finished?"

"Oh no," he said, "these things take time. But I'm delighted that you're done."

His typist was a pleasant motherly woman who also taught me to make Dutch apple strudel.

A few months later I found a publisher. Harold insisted on a celebration—we went to a very expensive restaurant for dinner, then on to a speakeasy near Trenton. Harold drank for the first time in months, and we both got light-headed and silly and had a snow fight on the front lawn of our little half-house, while the few remaining cats (most had wandered off or been trapped by our landlady) watched us from the security of the back porch. We tumbled inside and made frantic love, still wearing our coats and rubbers, on the living-room floor. My back ached for days. We both had frightful hangovers. And Harold lost a morning's work.

That spring, as the snows turned into rains and the first scraggly bits of green began to poke from the mud, Harold became more and more silent. More preoccupied.

He continued to work steadily, converting his notes into closely written pages. He kept them in a locked strongbox.

"It's fireproof," Harold said. "If the house should burn down we'd find the pages safe in the ruins."

"But not your notes." I pointed to the littered tables.

There was a flash of such dreadful fear in his eyes that I wished I'd kept silent.

"Yes"—his voice was steady, quiet—"they might also be stolen."

"Oh Harold, nobody will steal them. And I was joking about the fire. I was just being silly."

"It would be very easy to break in here." He ignored me. "It would be no problem at all to break in here."

That night we went to bed with all the lights burning, even in the bedroom. He insisted. "Put a pillow over your head if you need the dark."

He needed to see to protect his treasure.

Shortly after that he bought a shotgun and kept it, loaded, under the bed.

I thought it foolish and said so. "You do not know," he said. "You just don't know."

I decided to write another children's book, this time about my own childhood in Africa. I would have pictures too. I could draw well enough; children wouldn't have high aesthetic requirements. From memory I could sketch the shambas and the termite hills and the flame trees, the scornful Swahili, the Kikuyu and their herds.

I became as self-absorbed and preoccupied as Harold. I filled page after page of my sketchbook. And the more I recorded, the more I remembered.

I turned completely inward, I recorded images that had

lurked in my memory for years. I became as careless of time as Harold. I often forgot to cook, to shop. Harold never reminded me; he seemed glad to be relieved of the burden of food.

I couldn't stop. Like an alcoholic, I had to finish everything.

Finish. That was what I did. I selected the drawings, I wrote the simple text to accompany them. I mailed off the book and waited.

Harold was busier than ever. "I can't believe I'm this near the end," he said.

We had dinner with his mentor and friend, Professor Baylor Carmichael. He and Harold confidently discussed the possibility of jobs for the coming academic year. Harold wanted to join an expedition exploring the dye pits of Tyre. Professor Carmichael insisted that he needed teaching experience more than field work. They talked seriously about the University of Chicago—their graduate program should suit Harold very well. "Would you like to live in Chicago?" Harold asked, turning to me abruptly.

"Oh I'm sure I can live anywhere."

"Once you've lived in the bush you can live anywhere?" Professor Carmichael smiled benignly at me. I had given the right answer.

I didn't tell him that I hadn't lived in the bush but on a coffee plantation, that ravening animals hadn't threatened us, that the only enemies were monotony and isolation.

Let him read my book, I thought. I will send him a copy and maybe he will forget that it is for children and maybe he will read it, and then he will really know what life was like there.

Until then I would say nothing. Only smile agreement. He was important to Harold, so he was important to me.

Driving home, Harold seemed quieter than usual. "Aren't you happy?" I asked. "Aren't you pleased? It seems to me that everything is going splendidly."

"Yes." He sounded very tired. "There are so many decisions to make, so many choices."

I hurried my questions—I needed to know before we entered our house, and the inevitable events of the bedroom obscured everything else. "But you are pleased with the way things are going, aren't you?"

"I'm very pleased. Carmichael has been great and everything is fine."

¶ One month later, Harold Evans disappeared.

I'd been to the grocery—away no more than an hour—and he was gone. There was no message. All the lights were still burning, as they did while he worked, and there was a half-finished cup of tea in the kitchen.

At nine o'clock I called the hospitals, at ten the police.

And I waited. In the living room, staring at the ghostly dusting of white file cards like snowflakes. In the bedroom, stretched full length on the bed. In the kitchen, where I walked slowly up and down while the single remaining cat sat on the windowsill and watched me. At eleven o'clock I let her inside. She immediately climbed to the top of the rocking chair. Swaying slightly on the high back, she watched me with yellow-slitted eyes. I stared right back at her, unmoving.

I made a pot of tea and forgot to drink it. The phone did not ring, the cold damp night was perfectly quiet. It was a long time before I thought of the shotgun.

I lifted the bed covers, I put the lamp on the floor, I

stretched out flat on my stomach and looked. Carefully, behind each of the four legs. As if a shotgun were a small object
like a pearl that might have rolled into hiding there. The
polished hardwood boards were dustless and absolutely
empty. They gleamed faintly in the light. Even the exposed
coils of purple-painted bedspring above them seemed clean
and proper.

I'd had no idea I was such a good housekeeper.

I wanted to crawl under the bed, to hide. I'd never played
under beds when I was small. In Africa you were never sure
what sort of unpleasant thing you'd find in a dark corner.
The legs of our beds and tables and chairs stood in cans of
kerosene, moats to hold off the marauding insects. We lived
barricaded against them. They outnumbered us; they out-
lasted us with their patience and persistence. . . . We replaced mud floors with wood and they still found their way
past—devious, cunning, they would triumph over us yet. . . .

I stood up and put the lamp back on the table. Wondering:
*Why would Harold take the shotgun? What did he have to
do that would require a gun?*

I called Professor Carmichael. The phone rang a long time,
the operator cut in and out noisily, I could hear her sighing at
my insistence. Finally Professor Carmichael's voice came
on the line. "This is Lucy Evans," I said. "Is my husband
there?"

A long crackling pause. "Lucy Evans?"

"Yes sir," I said.

"Lucy Evans"—he cleared his throat—"it is one-thirty in
the morning."

"Yes," I said, "but do you know where my husband is?"

"Your husband," he said wearily patient, "is not here. I
have not seen him for at least a week."

I think I even stopped breathing for a minute or so, even my autonomic systems were staggered. I saw dancing black dots before my eyes and the black cord of the telephone squirmed like a snake.

"Mrs. Evans! Lucy Evans!" He was shouting into the phone and jiggling the receiver hook. "Operator! Operator!"

Of course the operator didn't come on. The few night girls had probably turned away from their boards to gossip.

"I'm here," I said finally.

"My dear child, your husband is an intense young man. He's overworked himself. He's gone for a long walk. That would be very much in character. A walk in the empty darkness. He'll be home when he gets tired—or realizes how silly the whole thing is."

"Yes," I said.

"He'll be contrite and apologetic in the morning." The voice was fatherly now. "Nothing to worry about. Go to bed, and I will too. . . ."

"Harold took a shotgun with him."

I could hear Professor Carmichael's breath go out in a long whistling sigh. "What?"

"He took a shotgun with him."

"My God," Professor Carmichael said slowly. "Have you called the police?"

"No accidents, they said. And nobody on their records sounded remotely like Harold."

"I didn't quite mean that . . . I'll call them myself. What was the gun for? Was it loaded?"

"Yes," I said. "Burglars."

He cleared his throat again. "I'll see what I can do."

The phone clicked down on his last word.

I needed a drink. In the kitchen cupboard I found an unopened bottle of Four Roses. Harold's father had given it to us—from his own carefully hoarded pre-Prohibition supply. He said: "You'll never see any more like this again."

Well, I would have some now. I poured a couple of inches and drank it neat.

The police came and we sat in the living room for a few minutes while I told them I hadn't the slightest idea where Harold had gone.

I'd no sooner closed the door than the phone rang—our landlady to tell me she was disgraced and ruined by the appearance of a police car outside her house at two-thirty in the morning.

I hung up without any comment. She did not call back, so I suppose she was satisfied by her own words.

I sat in the living room and stared at the stuccoed wall—at the swirls from a plasterer's trowel—until they squirmed before my eyes. I went to the kitchen and stared at the octagonal black-and-white tiles of the counter. I went into the bathroom and stared at the shelves of neatly folded towels. Because I was there, I took a bath, a long hot bubble bath. I changed to a blouse and skirt I particularly liked, a cornflower blue. The cat meowed and I opened the door to let her out. The night was chilly and damp and I shivered in the doorway. She hesitated. I scooped her up and tossed her out into the dark.

Eventually there was a faint lightening in the east and dogs began to bark sleepily and once I heard the half-completed crow of a rooster.

The greenish morning light grew like mold across the windows. I fixed coffee and drank it. I boiled an egg and scooped it neatly from its cup.

The phone rang and it was Professor Carmichael. The

phone rang and it was the police. The phone rang and it was Mrs. Carmichael saying that her husband had gone off to his office and I could reach him there. "It's so early for him," she said accusingly.

"It's early for me too," I said.

I brought in the morning paper from the front porch. As I stooped to pick it up, I noticed something white near the fence corner, close to the bare canes of the Seven Sisters rose bush. A piece of paper—probably a passing child had tossed a crumpled ball of schoolwork over the fence. I went to pick it up, tattered bits of paper look so messy.

After a few steps I saw that it wasn't paper. It was our cat. The entire side of its head had been crushed to a bloody pulp, with red trickles on the grass and a dangling eye and little smears of gray.

I'd put that cat out late last night. It was now early in the morning. No one was about at this hour—no child on the way to school, no neighbor on a casual stroll. Our landlady hated cats, but she could not do this. Who then?

I got newspaper and string. The cat had stiffened in the night chill and it was difficult to wrap and tie it securely.

Who would walk the streets before dawn? Who would kill a cat? Who could even approach this cat, a half-wild and wary animal?

And I heard Harold's voice, heard it so loudly that I spun around thinking he had come home.

"I don't like cats at all," he'd said. "Matter of fact, I loathe cats."

He'd been here last night. He'd been waiting.

The animal would come to him without fear. He'd fed them daily. It was he who adopted them in the first place. Protected them and fed them and killed them. . . .

Another idea crept into my mind. Came and stayed, half-expressed. The cat's death had averted mine. Harold had intended to kill me, and had killed the cat instead.

I put the wrapped animal in the garbage can. I went inside, locked the door, and sat quietly in a chair, shaking all over, like someone in a hepatic chill.

I remembered the saints' shrines I had seen in Italy, where the faithful leave tribute in the form of clay models. Hundreds of them jumbled together (with abandoned crutches): ears and arms and hands and legs, solid testimony to miraculous cures.

If I could find the proper saint and the correct shrine I would make an offering too, a small black-and-white cat. . . .

At mid-morning Professor and Mrs. Carmichael came to tell me that Harold was dead, a suicide.

"You must call his parents," Professor Carmichael said.

"I couldn't." Couldn't call up people I had hardly ever seen, didn't know, except through their son.

Something about the bearers of bad news being killed. . . .

He nodded. "I see."

What could he see, I wondered.

He went to the telephone, sitting so tall and thin and black on the corner table, surrounded by a sea of index cards. He called Harold's parents. I don't know what he said; I didn't listen. I was thinking: Harold is dead, and the cat is dead. Harold shot himself. And how do you shoot yourself with a shotgun? You have to have awfully long arms.

And over again: Harold is dead.

Automatically. As if I were trying to learn something by heart.

I did not disturb the file cards. I lived among them, among the other things that belonged to Harold. I only made a small clearing on the dining table by edging his cards closer together. I felt quite triumphant when I saw the little area of shiny wood appear.

I did not leave the house. There was enough food and I did not want to venture onto the streets where Harold had walked. I did not even glance at the corner of the yard where the cat had died. I closed my eyes whenever I had to look that way.

Two days later, the Evanses came, all of them, even the four brothers and their wives and their children. They filled the small rooms, they moved the furniture about, they ordered huge catered meals delivered in wicker baskets, they made immediate contact with a local bootlegger for a case of real Scotch. (They kept it under the small kitchen table; there was no other place to put it.) They were so noisy in their grief. They roared their anger at God.

They were surprised to hear that I had done nothing about the funeral. That isn't decent, my mother-in-law said, to leave Harold lying alone.

Though I couldn't see what difference it made, I said nothing. Their grief was so much more obvious than mine.

They planned the funeral; they organized with gusto and efficiency, washing everything with floods of tears.

I'd never seen men crying before.

The coroner had listed Harold's death as an accident, so we had a stately Episcopal service with solemn masses of flowers and a black cortège to the railroad (it was quite a long way) to put the coffin on the train west.

And all that time, they never once asked: Why?

As if they'd expected it.

I went back to Michigan with them, as was my duty. I had married Harold Evans; I wore his ring. I must go with him into that unknown country called the Middle West, that large expanse on my map (I had looked it up—I was unfamiliar with American geography). I must bury him in his familiar soil, completing what I'd contracted to do. You returned people to their beginnings. Harold would lie in a cemetery he knew, overlooking the town where he'd been born.

If I died, would anybody arrange for me to go back to Africa? Would I want them to? Where graves were dug extra deep because of hyenas? I did not care.

Harold now. Would he spend his eternity regretting that he had not finished with the file cards? Would he regret the cat? Would he regret not taking me with him?

His would be a restless grave, I was sure of that, the sort of grave that duppies hang about.

Africa was filled with duppies. I'd seen them myself. A five-foot rooster sauntering across the yard. A low white thing like a pig in the nighttime shadows.

When I looked across the cemetery in Ellis, Michigan, smooth and brown with the last of winter, I thought: *I am glad I do not live here, because there will be duppies for sure, and Harold will not rest; he will be looking for me. . . . Harold had loved me enough to want me to be buried with him. . . .*

I returned to our house in Princeton to finish Harold's book. I could not leave those notes unused.

I had to get a locksmith to open Harold's strongbox. The key had disappeared. Harold must have thrown it away. At least they didn't find it in his pockets.

The first part of the manuscript was neatly and professionally typed. The rest was handwritten pages, ending with an incomplete sentence. I stared at the last word Harold had written—the word was "westerly." I thought: *Harold ends here. This is the final demarcation of his spirit, this is the limit of his circle, beyond this it will be me.* Will any reader notice that one has ended and one begun?

When I put the first of my words to Harold's book, when I added one word to his final "westerly," I knew that he was truly dead. And I cried, for the first time, scalding hot tears. Love was not so common, and Harold's was gone.

Of course I pulled myself together and got on with the job. In a couple of months I was finished. The Press contracted to publish it and I wrote a proper dedication to Professor Carmichael. Then I closed the house, sold our furniture. The wedding gifts I returned to Harold's family—I sorted them out as best I could and with each one I sent the same note: *I know that Harold would want you to have this.*

And so out of my house went the crystal and the silver and the china; all the things that had come to me through the Evans family I returned to them.

I felt strongly about that: the presents had to be returned. As if I were burying them with his body in that vast Midwest I didn't know.

I think that Harold the archaeologist would have said that I was furnishing his grave with the proper supply of grave goods—to make his afterlife one of comfort and honor.

Perhaps in a way I was. The portion of pelf that had come with Harold returned westward with his body.

¶ I left Princeton one summer morning six months after Harold's death.

I locked the door on rooms stripped bare of everything that had been ours. A whiff of lemon oil followed me into the morning air.

I had been on a cleaning frenzy for two days. Every wall, every floor was washed and polished. My back ached and my hands were red and cracking, but there wasn't a fingerprint left. It was perfectly, hygienically, antiseptically, hospitally clean. . . .

The little cloud of lemon oil dissipated, leaving only the dust-tinged day around me.

I rang the landlady's bell. She came out immediately; she must have been waiting just the other side of the closed door.

"It's quite in order," I said.

"I'm sure," she said.

The taxi driver carried my baggage. Funny, how you could walk away from a marriage with only the contents of two not very large suitcases. Well, professional travelers always moved lightly, I assured myself.

In the cab I began checking the contents of my purse. Everything was there, of course. And in the bottom, with a jumble of hairpins and emery boards and a dusting of face-powder, was the charm I had carried since childhood. I took it out and looked at it. A beetle caught in yellow amber. Perfect and dead. When I was little I'd spent hours staring at it, rubbing it between my fingers. Trapped insect.

That was what I did all the everlasting ride to the Junction. It was what I did on the train to New York. Held my piece of amber.

I still have it. It has a drawer all its own in my jewel box, just above the big drawer that holds the beautiful garnets Stephen gave me.

Yes, Stephen. Stephen. I find it hard to believe that he is dead. I have to force myself to remember his funeral in the sun-blazed cemetery and the stone with his name.

Just the other day there was a phone call for him. "He's not here now," I said to them. "Shall I have him call you back?"

I wrote down name and phone number and then marked clearly: *Call back.*

I had completely forgotten.

I never had to force myself to remember that Harold was dead. I knew.

And I missed him. Those years in New York, I was very lonely. I worked hard in my classes at Barnard. (I was an oddity there: much older than the other girls, a widow.) I saw Harold's book through the press. The proofs were very difficult; there were so many diagrams—the printers made such foolish mistakes . . . but I finished it. Professor Carmichael wrote to me with the first copy: "This will be a classic. No doubt of it."

He was right. For years, until his death, Professor Carmichael sent me reviews as they appeared slowly in the scholarly quarterlies. Eventually, the reviews were succeeded by citations, little footnotes at the bottom of articles referring to Harold's work. "And this," Professor Carmichael wrote, "is a scholar's immortality."

So Harold had succeeded. In a way.

And so did I. In a way. My children's books let me refuse an allowance from Harold's family. And I did not need to return to my parents in Africa. They asked me to come. But I couldn't. Words from a Bible class in my childhood kept echoing: "There is no hope, no, for I have loved strangers and after them I will go."

Greenwood College, a women's school in Virginia, offered me a job. I had never heard of the school, I had barely heard of Virginia, but I said yes quickly.

The country was incredibly beautiful. The slopes and the hills were alive with their changing lights, their shifting colors. In Africa the land was a growing amorphous thing that obliterated all efforts of man on its surface; like a yeast dough that has grown monstrous, it absorbed all. It was eater and eaten, food and feeder. And featureless. In Virginia, there was always a face, sun and rain and snow.

¶ One Saturday evening I took four of my students to the Ansford Inn for a Unitarian colloquium. The title was "Man's Role in a Changing World: Ethics Today." These meetings were considered radical by my conservative college. I had to do a great deal of persuading before we were allowed to go.

Stephen Henley was at the meeting. He recognized me, introduced himself, and said that he had known Harold at Princeton.

"I've read your husband's book," he said. "It must have been a great deal of work for you to see it through."

He'd noticed the different hands, the seam in the book. That was perceptive of him.

"I needed work just then."

"It is a remarkably fine book," he said. And then, glancing at my four students who were standing as close by and listening as carefully as good manners allowed, "Do you teach?"

"At Greenwood College. Yes."

"A beautiful campus," he said. "I've often admired it. There is one particularly interesting building—a truly handsome old red brick house on a rise by the river."

"It's the only house in this part of the valley that survived the Civil War."

"I wonder why."

"It was used as a hospital, the story says. By the time the

wounded were evacuated, the main army was gone and the rear guard just didn't get around to firing it."

"Pure chance." His tone made those words the worst of insults. I found myself wishing that the lovely old house had burned rather than survive by chance.

"We should go. Girls!" They began moving slowly down the long steps to our parked car.

"I'm staying here at the inn," he said. "I've come down every spring since we started these meetings. It's a pleasant change from Shelby."

"Shelby?"

"Pennsylvania. Where my church is."

"Oh," I said.

"I'll be going back day after tomorrow," he said. "I drive through Greenwood."

He came, and we spent the late afternoon walking about the campus, admiring the different views of the valley. It was still chilly but the rhododendrons were blooming, and the dogwood and the wild azaleas. We went to five o'clock tea at the president's house. We met the retired president, an ancient lady, Miss Hilda Cornelia Lee. She had a doctorate from some German university, and she was a relative of Robert E. Lee. She was about ninety, very tall, very rawboned, very deaf. On this day she was wearing her velvet cloak. Everyone in the county knew that cloak; she had reportedly inherited it from her mother. It was rust-colored and lined with firm bright Stewart-plaid wool. (That had been added, people said, during the hard winter of 1919.) The outer velvet was decorated with elaborate embroidered flowers, joined by twisting tendrils of bright green. Supposedly Miss Lee embroidered around each new moth hole, turning each flaw into a bright-colored flower. In the fall you might see a new bouquet among the faded sprays—an indication that she had been careless in her off-season storage.

Stephen was very patient and very diplomatic with her. He was obviously used to handling old people. I told him so.

"I'm an old man myself," he said easily. "That's all."

¶ I got the first of his letters the following week—the first in a long series that stretched across the summer and through the following academic year. He occasionally came to visit, but the train connections were poor and the roads uncertain.

It was a great relief for both of us when we finally married.

My mother came to the wedding. That short dumpy woman with a large white front like a pigeon had not changed at all. She'd been visiting her sister in England when my letter arrived and had immediately decided to come for the ceremony. "After all," she said, "I was halfway here already." If you started from Africa, England was indeed halfway to Greenwood, Virginia. Distance meant nothing to my mother. She had special clothes for traveling—all dust-colored, khaki-colored, except for a small green hat which could be secured against the weather by lashings of green veiling.

My mother arrived at Greenwood two days before the wedding, and there was a great rush to meet her. (I suspect they thought that anyone from Africa must be black.) My mother loved it. She knew that people were studying her—and having trouble with her accent—and she was enjoying every minute. She was also studying them with great curiosity. Virginia was as much a foreign country to her as Africa would have been to them.

She surveyed the town's enormously wide main street—
which was quite empty except for a few parked cars at Miller's
Rexall Drugs and two trucks outside Graham's Feed Store.
"Whatever happened to the town?" she said.

"I suppose it didn't grow as much as people thought."

"It would look nice," my mother said, "if they put a park
in the middle. Your father would have some ideas about it."

Yes, I thought, my father would. He had the soul of a
nineteenth-century gentleman. Had he been able to afford
it, he would have decorated his African landscape with de-
caying castles and secret grottoes and ruined choirs.

We went to the drugstore—my mother must have some
aspirin—and had a long talk with Mr. Miller. Mr. Harder,
who published the semi-weekly paper, came in to ask if there
was anything he could add to his social column. We went to
the bakery and my mother sniffed the air with approval. We
went to the bank and, as we were leaving, we met Mr.
Ormond. He was from South Carolina, one of the few people
in town who was not a native. He was also the undertaker.

"Oh," my mother said. "We have very few of you people
in Africa. Except for Europeans, nobody really bothers to
bury, you see."

Mr. Ormond looked doubtful.

"The Kikuyus take dying people out of their huts—if
they died inside they'd have to burn the whole thing down
and they really don't want to do that. So they carry them out
in the bush and they just leave them there. It's very efficient
and clean, you know, and it feeds the hyenas and keeps them
away from the stock."

Mr. Ormond retreated into the bank, hastily. "Mother, I
think you shocked him."

"Nonsense," she said firmly, "how can you shock an undertaker?"

¶ After the wedding my mother left for New York and the ship back to England. She was most at home with a suitcase clutched in each hand and an umbrella hanging from her arm.

Stephen and I, without pausing for a honeymoon, went home to Shelby—knobby coal-rich hills and stone-littered slopes, thinly covered by green in summer; the town built in a deep hollow so that its twisting streets ran like rivers through the bottom of a canyon; a shadowy place where tall narrow houses clustered together like stalagmites growing from a cave floor. . . . We moved into one of those houses, narrow, two-storied, green with brown trim. We lived there for thirty-four years.

Until Stephen retired.

Only then did the meanness and ugliness and smallness of the town oppress me. I had not noticed it before.

Stephen felt no difference. He was startled when I suggested we move. He agreed: "If it's important to you."

I read book after book on Florida. I got maps from the AAA office and studied them carefully. And the more I read, the more I longed for the warmth of palmetto flats. I discovered Silver Shores, Florida. It was a small town directly on the Gulf, low white houses and blue sky, sandy ground, pine trees like toothpicks, oleanders towering over my head, and yellow hibiscus flowers larger than my hand. I found a house. We moved.

I planned the change with as much precision and care as I could. The house in Pennsylvania must be folded and packed away into barrels and boxes and then be unfolded and fitted into the palm trees of Florida. I think I did that fairly well; I even managed to keep much the same arrangements of furniture—so that Stephen would not be unnecessarily disturbed.

As soon as Stephen arrived, he sent a photograph of the house to his father. "He will not like it, of course."

And then his father was on the telephone saying, in that high precise voice of his, "You have managed to find a house even uglier than the one in Pennsylvania. A triumph!"

Our moving infuriated him. Stephen showed me one letter. "She has carried you off to her lair," his father wrote, "and she'll devour you there like the Black Widow spider. My dear boy, you are only discovering what I found out before you, and all men before us. Women get you at the last. For a while you think you have them, with their soft bodies and their beckoning distances that lure you on as if there were something waiting for you. But you grow tired and they don't, and in the end they have got you. Look at me now. Nurses, goddamn nurses. I shall be carried to my grave by women. Clotho and Agapos and Atropos—women again, measuring your life."

And Stephen said, "I'm always amazed at how well read that man is." But he did not really deny the substance of his father's thought. . . .

Stephen changed. Slightly, subtly.

But he was not unhappy; I am sure he was not unhappy.

¶ Now, without Stephen, I know what it is to be truly alone, to listen to all the busyness inside my own head. All the random buzzings and creakings.

If the phone rings, I do not have to answer. There is no one

I care about, no one I need worry about. My sons have their wives and each other. In emergencies they will take care of themselves, they will not need me. There is nothing I must do. If I do not feel hungry, I do not fix supper. If I want nothing but jellied eggs for a week (how Stephen disliked them), then I have jellied eggs. I follow my own tastes, my own instincts.

Like a hermit crab in the shelter of my house. White cinderblock. It does seem rather like the cast-off shell of some square undersea creature.

¶ After Stephen's death, after my sons left, I grew panicky. What if something should go wrong, I thought.

And I finally answered: What could happen? What could possibly happen to you? Everything horrid and evil has already happened. What else is there? You could die. And would you mind? Would you really mind? And the answer drifted by so clearly: *Not really.*

I stopped being afraid. You are only afraid when you have something to lose, something you want to hold on to, something you value. I had nothing like that.

I began to enjoy the silence: the knowledge that there was no breathing inside the walls but mine. If I held my breath, if I stopped that steady in-and-out rasp, there would be absolute quiet.

It amused me sometimes to hold my breath and to pretend that I had died and to experience what the house would be like then. The absolute motionless quiet. . . . Until, I told myself nastily, the house was sold and some old couple quarreled their way through the rooms.

Oh I wasn't sentimental. Old women are supposed to

quake with an excess of emotion—perhaps love—and start talking to animals and birds and flowers on the windowsill. I didn't. Matter of fact, I could feel myself firming and hardening, as if I were developing emotional muscles. I began to feel that I could look more directly at things than ever before. Old clear-eyed beady-eyed Cowboy Me, straightest glance in the West. . . .

I felt that for the first time in my considerably long life I was seeing things truly. I began to see that I was born to be old.

I may even marry again. (Stephen's father seems to have guessed correctly.) His name is Carter Hollins; he retired from the insurance business some years ago. We play golf three or four times a week, we go out to dinner at least twice.

But I am not sure I want to marry again.

Because now I have freedom. If I want to go for a drive at three in the morning, there is no one to argue about it. I take the car keys and I go. I drive along the beach and stare across the Gulf, wondering if I see the same horizon that pirates saw four hundred years ago.

Or the rangers. They were Caribbean fishermen who ranged about isolated islands for weeks on end, hunting the big sea turtles. Day after day, living with the empty horizon. Wondering if the boat that had left them would pick them up before their water was gone.

How would they see the horizon? With sun-scorched days and star-scorched nights and a knowledge that whatever happened would come from the sea?

There was no one to laugh at my fantasy of pirate and ranger.

There was no one to be happy with me, you say? The contented chuckle, the community of joy?

There was no one, true. But there was no occasion either. No great joys to celebrate. No fear to comfort.

There was, at times, a gentle amusement. And there was often a sense of contentment. Of peace. Or of readiness, if you want to be Shakespearean.

Over my days and nights there was a kind of smooth lacquer-like surface. A kind of invisible moonlight.

¶ I am content. I have come halfway around the world and I feel at home. I was born on the dusty high plains of Africa and I end my life watching the Gulf of Mexico.

Stephen of course was never at home anywhere. Without his restless presence, his silent crackle of scholarly scheming and analyzing, I am more peaceful than before.

The phone rings now and I consider answering it.

If it stops before I make up my mind—no loss.

I do not need the message of the electronic voice.

I need very little. Not sex. Not the way I once needed Harold's body—the very thought of that time leaves me shuddering. Not a husband. Not sons.

I suppose I need silence; I need emptiness.

I am content.

¶ Paul's voice, angry and hurt. "Why don't you answer the phone, Mother? We only worry about you because we love you."

God save me from love. And the proof of love.

Years ago with Harold, I waited longing, lusting. I watched him finish work, close his book carefully, marking his place with a bit of red construction paper, and put his pen in its green onyx holder. Only then he remembered desire and his need for a woman's body.

As we made our orderly and unhurried progress to the bedroom, I was quivering. Actually. My hands were not steady. I learned to hold the glass with two hands when I rinsed my brushed teeth.

Dear Lord, how I remember the pleasure and the pain and the satiety. The incredibly heavy feeling of exhausted legs, the aching chest, the sweet taste in my mouth.

All that was evidence of love.

And Stephen. Whom I married in boredom and desperation. With whom I lived in the coal-dusted hills of Pennsylvania, in a tall narrow house like a myopic vision. And I was happy. Oh yes. Stephen's bed was quiet and loving and somehow reminded me of the outdoors—not only because of the lavender I kept in the linen closet. Stephen had the logic of nature.

Something like that. It is hard to talk about it, any of it. It is hard to find the right words. I admire Stephen and I love him, and if there is that Christian heaven of reunion, I will join him with joy. Harold? Oh Harold will never be found in a Christian heaven. He belongs to an earlier time. He himself is one of the travelers on those ancient trade routes he studied so carefully. A sailor, perhaps, with a cargo of cedars from Lebanon, overdue and bound for Egypt.

He will be with them. Where he belongs.

¶ Do I think much about the afterlife, the other world? Much less now than when I was younger. Since I shall have the answer fairly soon, I've rather lost interest in the question.

In the meantime, my days turn as smoothly as glass. I

walk easily through my remaining time, my bones ache only slightly, my vision is only slightly impaired and I still hear quite well. Almost everything amuses or interests me. Just the other day I watched dust spin in a fall of sunlight. I watched by the hour.

EDWARD

MILTON

HENLEY

¶ Tedious. So miserably tedious. I really ought to have swallowed those twelve Seconals long ago, when my fingers could still pick them up, when my legs could still carry me to the bottle.

No more. Now I reach it only with my eyes, that squat square bottle among all the others neatly grouped in the corner. (Amazing how many medicines keep me alive.) Too far away. My legs no longer support me, my shoulders are no longer strong enough to lift me from the bed.

These good people, these ministering angels with their ridiculous lacy caps and their white starched coats, they have only one purpose—to keep me alive.

Pity.

So it remains tedious. Yes. And confusing.

I see a window, a bright sunlit window. I call the orderly for a wheelchair tour of the garden—when I notice that the window is not sunlit at all but holds the blank empty reflection of night. Did it change while I was looking at it—could I have watched the change? Did I sleep? How many hours have passed? Or perhaps the window was never bright at all, I only perceived it as such. Or perhaps it was never dark.

That is only one measure of the confusion I find myself confronted with.

I can never remember the date, neither day, month, nor year. Despite this, every morning after breakfast, I read the newspapers—I have a stand for them, my hands are too unsteady. My white-hatted guardian stands next to me and when I nod, she turns the page. I could manage that myself, but very slowly. Better to let this hired angel do it for me.

For all my organization, I retain very little of what I have just read. What I do remember are newspapers from years past. Remember them as if they were this morning's front page.

I've just finished reading the *Times*. Not strange, you say. But the date was April 1912, and the headlines concerned the *Titanic* disaster. There was a newly revised list of the missing. I scanned it quickly: Mr. and Mrs. Roger M. Butterworth, Chicago. My sister and her husband. I quivered with shock and disbelief. My totally protected sister was lost in the north Atlantic, her bones would be swaying forever in those dark obscure currents.

Ah yes, those currents. That hold all the dead men and the dead ships for hundreds and thousands of years. That dive beneath continents and rise again. Might I not find my sister in the flow of White Springs, Virginia, say, or discover her thoroughly boiled in Hot Springs, Arkansas? Would a steward's cap from the *Titanic* appear one day in the Mississippi? Would a bit of a German U-boat sail again on the Red River or the *Bismarck* cruise in tiny miniature splendor on the Hudson?

It was not that she was my only sister—due to the circumstances of our upbringing and the difference in our age I hardly knew her. But the whole thing was out of character, so totally out of character for her.

That sense of outrage I felt when I read the headline —was it this morning? It seems so fresh, so immediate.

My nurse, her white starched bib rustling, asks, "Don't you remember this morning's paper? Don't you remember about President Ford?"

Testing. Testing. Plumbing the depths of my senility.

Actually I did not remember anything about President

Ford. Oh I had read something, but that was years ago. Or was it?

What a bore all this is for me.

¶ But I am not lonely. I have a great many visitors, who seem to come without regard for time. This morning—the window was gleaming bright and I was in my wheelchair ready to go into the garden—Ernst Freyhausen bounded through the door, cheerful as ever. With him he brought the smell of Berlin streets, dust and manure and perfume mixed in a certain proportion. Ernst was killed in 1917, of course, but there we sat, laughing together. He was always a great one for jokes and stories of his women, and his accent, which started sounding strange to my ear, ended by not sounding like an accent at all and his German ceased to be a foreign language and became as clear to me as my English words. His father, he told me, was furious with him, suspecting him of infecting a mistress who had transmitted the disease to his father. It meant a long course of mercury for both. *Not me,* Ernst said. *I have never touched her,* he said, *I am as pure as the driven taxi cab.* He slapped his knee like a peasant, threw back his head and roared with laughter. The daylight glinted on the scar across his cheek, the bright liver-colored dueling scar. . . .

My grandsons come, both of them, and their wives and children. *How are you, Grandfather, the children especially want to say hello this trip, Grandfather.* (Little ones with faces either bored or scared.) Once they brought a German nanny with them, and for a few minutes Ernst floated in the background, sliding back and forth on the gutturals of her speech.

My son Stephen comes too, of course. Stephen would always come; Stephen was always correct. He sits and talks politely, not too long, not enough to tire me.

And I don't tell him that I have seen his funeral in a white sand graveyard, have the film stored in my library, suitably marked and catalogued. I keep a secretary for just that sort of thing.

Lucy comes. Prim homely Lucy. "Stephen was here," I tell her. "What day was it? Yesterday perhaps. You must ask the ogre."

The ogre smiles and nods her white-capped head.

"Stephen is dead, Father."

"Stephen was *here*. . . ." Foolish woman, how could I tell her any more plainly.

My own father stops by—briefly—dressed for a summer croquet afternoon, white flannels and straw boater.

My mother comes too, saying as she did so many years ago, "The doctors say the boy is dying. We must put the parlors into order this very minute."

¶ How busy my death is. And how slow.

My body, consider that. I was once tall, and I have shrunk by some three inches. I had myself measured some years ago, when I was still able to stand—I had indeed diminished. I am curling like a leaf shriveling as it disappears into dust.

I notice these things dispassionately.

Consider also my world. I am limited to this house, this room. It is, to be sure, a rather fine room in the best nineteenth-century tradition. That wreath of plaster acanthus leaves surrounding the chandelier—extraordinary craftsmanship. I have spent hours studying it, admiring the skill of the man who made it.

He also comes to see me—or it. In his workman's smock, dusty with plaster, polite and deferential in the manner of artisans a century ago, he bows to me and stands a little to one side, contemplating his work. Once he nodded to me and said: Best one I ever did make, sir. Another time he brought a ladder and climbed up to it, to adjust the curve of a leaf that did not please him.

One of my nurses walked through the edge of the ladder, knocking him sideways, so that he staggered and almost lost his balance. He said politely: The ladies don't notice, sir. And that is a very fine piece of work.

There is so little we can talk about. I ask him if he worked on my father's house. He looks shocked. No sir, he says, they used only masters and I was just an apprentice in those days.

Pity. I would have enjoyed hearing about that.

But never mind. I have other things to entertain me, other events to fill my days.

My world is this room, impressive but small, and in good weather the garden.

A lovely garden, its walls bright pink with espaliered apple blossoms in spring.

But little. Pathetically little.

When frost begins to turn the bricks moldy with its glaze, I leave this house for an Arizona hilltop. My winter terrace, sheltered by a Plexiglas wind screen lest I be blown into irreparably damaged pieces, overlooks a desert. Or so they tell me. A vast expanse I can no longer see. My vision has dimmed. I am fit only for my enclosed terrace. . . .

I do not tolerate well so small a world.

I feel I am being crowded off the earth's surface. At any moment the last foothold will be whipped from under me, like the rug in a vaudeville joke.

I do not care to wait much longer.

I have read that on slave ships of the last century, certain perfectly healthy males would tell their fellows that they were going to die, would stand, and with a great shout fall dead. Suicide without weapons. A tremendous contraction of muscles, perhaps, a vast increase of pressure against the heart.

I see them now in my imagination, those shining black men, with their expanded chests and their final dying shouts. . . .

I have never had a black man. Black women, of course, in all their splendid skin tones. One in Rio whose skin was the only truly golden color I have ever seen, far brighter and more gleaming than the dull yellow of the Oriental. (Oriental women have always seemed to me vastly overrated. I dislike the yellow stain their skin leaves on the bed linen. Their tiny bones, their narrow pelvises seem inadequate and unhealthy to me. I have always preferred a certain robustness in my women.) But the golden Negroes, how beautiful they are—that woman in Rio even had golden eyes. A magnificent animal. Another, in Jamaica, was so black her skin shone blue in the light; she had a bulge to the back of her skull and a loose-jointed walk that translated perfectly into the bedroom.

But never a black man. I wonder why.

With foolishness like this I fill my days. While longing for the release in that bottle of Seconal. Across the room, across the ocean. One and the same for me.

¶ My grandson Paul arrives. Again with that canvas under his arm, that drab portrait of an ancient woman, heavy and dull with years. He is convinced that it is his grandmother.

Whenever he is announced, Nurse Robertson's eyebrows go up. She glances at me to see if I will spare us all by saying: "I am tired, tell him not today." But I do not. Paul and his foolish picture come in the door as Mrs. Robertson nods and leaves. The changing of the guard.

Quite soon, because he feels my powers of concentration are failing, Paul displays his picture. "Doesn't she look familiar to you, Grandfather?"

"Why should she look familiar to me?"

It is a game we play, he and I. Same questions, same answers. Eventually one of us may forget his lines. Does truth then lie in blunders? Can we uncover something by our mistakes that was hidden to our earnest endeavors?

I think that is probably quite true, probably even the nature of the world we find ourselves in.

"Could this be the woman who bore my father?"

I look at his ugly picture again, just to please him. The boy is so serious. . . . Why don't I just lie and say yes and have him go away happy?

Why don't I? I have no aversion to lying. Oh no. But to lie about this would create many more problems. For Paul at least. (Death will solve all mine.) He would immediately acquire a host of cousins, and he would worry about them all.

"Paul," I say, "did you actually have the gall to ask that old woman if she ever had any illegitimate children?"

"Of course not, Grandfather. But why would she give me this picture if she didn't feel something special for me?"

"You were a buyer," I say wearily. "I have too much

experience with the ways of sellers not to recognize the pattern when it presents itself."

He goes back to the picture again, pointing out the house that was very much like my house, the corbeled arches, the horses' heads.

How tiresome, tiresome.

"My dear boy, I last saw the woman who bore your father some sixty-odd years ago. How could I recognize her?"

"But some feeling, some sense of what you had had together?"

"Pisswillie," I said, recollecting a phrase that had been very much in vogue in my youth.

And I fell asleep on him.

¶ Pitiful. That handsome slender well-dressed man is consumed by his search for the great mother figure, the earth goddess, life-giver to us all.

I had a woman like that once, I forget where, a huge woman with reddish hair and hips that must have been two years across. She was so deep, I had the sensation of falling. Quite exhilarating. I went to her often until the novelty died. Novelty and love are the same thing. To me.

Not of course to Paul. I have heard him on the subject often enough to understand his position perfectly.

My super-rational son Stephen and his well-organized Lucy produced this foolishness, this man-child who craves the pursuit and capture of love.

¶ Wearisome. Tedious. More and more often I find myself watching that beautiful bottle. Watching as if my eyes could draw it to me across the room. . . .

I even rehearse my actions. I have the capsules in my mouth. I count them as I swallow, one, two, three, four, five, six, seven. Enough. Then the soft chilling. I recognize it. I have a taste of it every night. The fingers that grow cold, the eyelids that grow heavy, the sleep that really does come like a sigh (despite the cliché) on barbital-feathered wings. The final sleep.

I wait for it.

I am only waiting for it. In insufferable boredom, in gentility and sobbing-end nonsense, I await my final dissolution. I have never been a patient man. As you may imagine, I do this badly.

¶ Other people come. My grandson Thomas. Square flushed face, beard-shadowed. He has brought his two sons. Overgrown and noisy, they sit in a far corner and pretend they are not here.

I know how they feel. I often went with my mother on her interminable calls. Down streets smelling of horses and up stone steps into houses smelling of wax and lavender. And sticky cakes which I refused to eat. . . .

I must have my housekeeper locate some such dreadful cakes. These boys must also have the pleasure of refusing them.

We move into the garden, nameless red-knuckled hands push my chair. Thomas walks ahead with his boys.

In the garden, in the filtered sun of my special corner, I can smell the tree roses and that very sweet low-growing gardenia. Its star flowers are right at my feet.

"And how is Claudia?"

Thomas bounces out of his chair, spins back and forth

across the small garden. The flowers shake, the stones shiver. Or so it seems.

"She left me."

He walks up and down again and stops directly in front of me. "That bitch left me."

The two boys giggle. But say nothing in defense of their mother.

I imagine Thomas in his present mood would knock them over.

"Grandfather, she left a note on the kitchen table, the *kitchen* table."

There are at least six gardenias within reach of my cane (oh yes, I still carry a cane even though I no longer leave my chair). I poke at them, trying to hit each yellow eye.

Thomas drops into a chair, it shivers beneath his considerable weight but does not break.

"Do you know what she said? That she's had a guy for the last year and leaving's been on her mind all that time. And I can have the boys because she's on her way to Caracas with him."

"Strong feelings," I say to the gardenia. "I knew Caracas fifty years ago, there was very little to it then. What does he do?"

Thomas hesitates, then with a brief hair-tearing gesture: "Boys . . . what does the bastard do?"

From out of sight an answer: "City water systems."

Whatever that meant. He built them or blew them up, I suppose. One or the other.

"She said I was so fat I was repulsive. Her word. Repulsive. And her with a Caesarean like a barn door."

Ah well. It is surprising the things people put in farewell letters.

My Eleanor, for example. "You disgusting satyr," she wrote. I felt rather flattered by the identification. I didn't think I quite made the grade, but I was willing to try. And the woman (who was it?) who dumped a scuttle of coal on my bed cover, and in the dust traced large words: Fuck you. Coal dust is so greasy, the bed was ruined, but so, I imagine, was her dress.

And then there was that boy, that little queer boy I picked up one night at the theater. Doubtless he was cruising the lobby looking for someone like me. Ah well, I too was looking, I suppose, though I was not aware of it. (I have always found sex more enjoyable if not planned like a travel schedule.) Frightful boy, wasn't even very clean in his personal habits, as my mother would have said. In the morning I went to work (I have always worked quite hard, a latent lingering bit of Protestant Ethic), leaving instructions with my staff to feed the boy breakfast and have him out of the house within an hour. I did not like the idea of various household articles disappearing—he had been paid quite well. Despite the watchful care of my butler and valet, that annoying boy contrived to slip away into my library. There he took down one of my shotguns, loaded it, and as the pursuit (which now included the chauffeur) burst through the door, fired—not at them, but into the wall. He'd only loaded with number nine birdshot, but he still managed to shatter two windows and ruin a very fine Braque which I had bought not a week before. The three men wrestled the gun away, hustled him outside and literally threw him down the stairs and into the gutter. But the damage was done. The picture was shredded. Though I had it repaired, I never liked it again. I finally sold it to a small museum at a very low price; they seemed quite happy with their bit of stitched and patched canvas. The gun he had used (a magnificent engraved Purdy, made to my measure) I simply gave away. I no longer wanted to handle it.

⁋ I myself have never indulged in such demonstrations of anger. I've never so much as written a farewell letter. When love ends, both parties are aware of it. Any form of notification is quite superfluous.

Yet many people do feel compelled to make a scene. Like Claudia—that foolish woman had obviously upset Thomas. Too bad. I've always found Thomas the more charming of my grandsons, perhaps because I purport to see evidence of my character in his. But not this. I do not think I ever regretted the loss of a love.

"Thomas"—it is really a considerable effort for me to talk—"Claudia will come back."

He rocks forward in his chair until his nose almost touches mine. He's been drinking; bourbon is heavy on his breath. "You think so, you think maybe so?"

His blue eyes are sunk in a tangle of red veins, there are dark circles across his cheeks.

"I think she'll come back."

"Bitch!" There seems to be onion mixed with the bourbon. "I hope to hell she does come back because it would give me the goddamndest pleasure to throw her out."

I smile at him then, though a smile is one of the most exhausting gestures I can make. He is very like me after all.

⁋ But he would not give me the Seconal I so ardently desire. I do not ask him because I know he will not. Because in his way he loves me.

❡ Then came a great number of cloudy days—although I am never sure whether the obscurity exists outside the windows or within the shelter of my skull.

There is rain streaming down the panes. Or perhaps it is tears across the lenses of my own eyes.

Things become one and the same. And that is alternately comforting and upsetting.

❡ There is talk of winter and the approach of cold weather. The pyracantha in my garden grows heavy with red berries, its clubbed shape stretching across the brick wall above the brilliant yellow chrysanthemums.

The tailor comes to fit me for my winter clothes, white flannels and blue blazers. The shirtmaker too. This winter I will affect the tucked and pleated shirt.

They are, of course, dressing a corpse.

An impatient corpse.

My measurements have changed drastically since last year. The tailor denies it. The prices of his suits oil his tongue into subtle flattery.

Deliberately difficult, I insist on putting on a blazer I wore last year. It hangs from my shoulders like a man's coat on a boy. The tailor does not blink an eye. He assures me that the coat has been stretched by the cleaners. His measurements from last year show no change at all, nothing to indicate that I am growing smaller and smaller.

Perhaps, I say, I am actually growing slightly larger, a rather delayed adolescence.

Even that outrageous statement does not upset him. It is quite possible, he says, that he applied his tape measure a trifle loosely last year and that my measurements are, in truth, slightly larger this year.

I order a suit of brilliant pink silk surah. Still his face does not move. (I will of course never wear that suit. I shall only occasionally refer to it.)

But I grow weary of my games. I have teased and mocked so much during my life that I have exhausted the amusement to be found therein.

I am tired; breathing is wearisome.

I search for an escape.

On all sides there are paid professionals devoted to keeping me alive. Their equipment fills my house—defibrillator and respirator and oxygen tank and God knows what else in their life-support system. All discreetly concealed, all waiting. The linen closet has become a pharmacy, its shelves neatly lined with bottles and instruments.

Everything to keep me alive and breathing in this bed. To keep me locked inside this body which is crumbling all around me. I marvel each day that my ribs do not simply collapse, like the roof timbers of some deserted house. Even if that did happen, I suspect they would merely produce a giant pump and pneumatically restore me to my former shape. . . .

I must sneak away from them then; I must seek and find my way to safety.

The prospect elates me, reminds me of those summers when, as child, I hid from my nurses in the brambly woods behind the stables. . . .

One day I will hide from these good people too, and they will never find me. . . .

Then what? After death what? A place of vague spirits and lights? No.

I have been there, I think. Fifty years ago, when I was still comparatively young, I hunted jaguar in Mexico. I was avid for trophies in those days, tigers in India, elephants in Africa, a grizzly in Canada, most dangerous of all. . . . But this jaguar hunt in Mexico. There were five or six Mexican guides and I alone. We stopped at a village for fresh fruit. On the way back to our camp, the chief guide showed me what he'd also bought—he pulled it from under his shirt, an ugly brown-stained and not very clean pipe. The entrance to heaven, he said.

We—all of us—smoked it. A single puff, pass it on. The first puff was extremely unpleasant—unfamiliar and very irritating. The smell was a bit like the undersides of rotting logs. The taste seemed to be rather like cinnamon. Or was it cloves? But unpleasant. Most astringently unpleasant. The second time the pipe came around the taste was less objectionable, it seemed to have developed a touch of cilantro. . . . After the third puff (all that I remember having), with a sudden twitch and jerk, I left my shell self. I lay, I walked, I floated in a gleaming smooth world. No trees, no bushes, no people, I bounded across the surface of a world as bare and shiny as a billiard ball. I danced with gods who lurked in the windless air around me. I was perfect, complete. Like a circle. There was only light without glare, and motion without movement.

How long? Who knows. I finally returned to a camp that reeked of vomit and excrement.

The vision lingered—I had been to heaven.

I tried to return—the pipe was gone and the guides denied ever seeing one. In my rage, I threatened them with my rifle, only to find it unloaded. My legs shivered and collapsed. I poured with sweat, streams ran down my arms and soaked into the ground. I fell into a sleep as solid and abrupt as an anesthetic.

Over the years I have tried other drugs. I even once went to Lima for a particularly famous brew of cocaine and coconut milk. But none was the gate to heaven.

Still, I have seen it. I have seen it.

The memory has given substance to these my days, the memory of clarity in confusion.

¶ Lucy, my daughter-in-law, visits me. She sits by the bed and talks. I barely listen to her.

Until she suddenly offers: "Would you like the Seconals? Would you like me to give you the Seconals?"

I come full awake at her words. "Yes."

"I'll put them in your hand," she said, "but you'll have to take them yourself."

Could I do that? And who was she to exact conditions from me?

Alas, her muscles still coordinated properly, her legs still functioned, she was not held prisoner by a corps of white-coated nurses. . . .

And so she could indeed demand conditions from me, who once would have laughed at her.

Now she is my escape. An angel visiting me.

"You take three grains every night," she says briskly, as if reporting the weather, "so you have probably developed a tolerance. Eight or ten, I would think."

She puts two capsules in my hand. With considerable trembling my hand reaches my mouth; she holds the glass of water. So slowly, so very slowly. She puts four more in my palm. "Is that too many?" she asks.

I do not answer. I concentrate on those red capsules.

"I will wait," she says. "As long as I am here, the nurse will not return. She will never notice that anything is wrong."

How efficient of her. How very efficient to think of such details. I feel a twinge of uncertainty, regret. But no, I will not let this foolish woman spoil the plan for my entrance through the gate of heaven into that brilliant light.

As I wait to die, my mind seems unusually active and clear. (At least compared to its state during these past years.) As I suppose one must, I try to sum up my life. It is very difficult, the words do not seem to fit the thoughts.

I seem to be trying to speak in a language I do not know.

I have left a will. I really ought to have left an epitaph. It would say: Here lies one who laughed at his own jokes his entire life long.

Yes, that would be nice. And so very accurate.

That is exactly what I have done. Amuse myself. Or have I done anything more? My son Stephen would say, as he did say once, that I was seeking the truth that is beyond satiation and exhaustion. "Your truth, Father, is the road of the Dionysiacs," he told me once.

This skin is wearing, is fraying, to me.

Stephen was always looking for the significance of things.

The unexamined life is not worth living, he would quote to me. He had a taste for tired aphorisms. Curious. Because he was actually, I heard, an extremely competent scholar. But with me, at least, he chose to hide his learning behind dullness. Will he still be doing that when I see him again, I wonder. Will he be waiting behind that blaze of infinity to offer me some trite observation?

It has grown quiet in here. Absolutely quiet. Am I now dead? I see quite well. There is Lucy, she sits reading a maga-

zine at my bedside. I see the title: *House and Garden.* I see
her turn the pages, but I hear nothing.

She stands up now and puts aside the magazine. She looks
at me, carefully, for a long time, there is no expression in
her face. How old she looks, how tired, with deep crease
lines along her nose, boxing in the mouth, scoring the chin.

Old woman. My own mother never looked so old. She
would never have let herself look so old.

I feel quite light, quite comfortable. The itching and fraying of my skin has ceased.

Lucy still stands looking at me. Not an impolite stare. A
watchful, penetrating, patient gaze.

Except for her the room is quite empty. I glance around
it, carefully examining the corners. Empty.

The dead who have visited me during these last months—
where are they now? I thought they might gather to welcome
me to their midst.

They were here in such numbers before.

Lucy walks to the window and stands looking out.

There is beginning to be a rather greenish light in this
room. A thickening glow, it seems to be sagging down from
the ceiling.

Something like that old-fashioned mosquito netting you
once saw everywhere.

Lucy leaves the window and comes to look at me again.
I wink and smile at her, but she gives no answer. Strange.
What has happened to her? I speak to her now, I say: Lucy!
And again: Lucy! She does not seem to hear.

She walks away toward the door. She seems to be calling
the nurse.

No, Lucy. Too soon, too soon. They will haul me back to

life. I must be dead, completely dead. I must slip through that gate of heaven.

The nurse, the orderly, the maid too, hurry in only to stop abruptly just inside the doorway. They stand staring, surprise on their faces. They whisper to each other, bending mouth close to ear. The orderly makes the sign of the cross—when I was a child I had a nurse who did that every single time she heard thunder. In summers her right arm was always flying about.

The pale green glow hangs more deeply from the ceiling, Lucy's head brushes it as she walks over to the phone.

The maid wipes away a tear. Thinking of her next job no doubt, which won't be half as easy as this one.

Still it is nice to be missed. Any way. In any fashion.

I am dead then. And why do I continue to see these people? I am, I suppose, flickering like a lightbulb. There is just enough energy in my neurons, enough sputtering of current. Like a battery running low.

That once in Mexico, the dirty caked pipe and the ineffable glory that followed. The gate of heaven, the life beyond death, the way the drug showed me. The taste of paradise, the perfect union. It must be here. Here.

A NOTE ON THE TYPE

The text of this book was set on the Linotype in Garamond No. 3, a modern rendering of the type first cut by Claude Garamond (1510–1561). Garamond was a pupil of Geoffroy Tory and is believed to have based his letters on the Venetian models, although he introduced a number of important differences, and it is to him we owe the letter which we know as old style. He gave to his letters a certain elegance and a feeling of movement which won for their creator an immediate reputation and the patronage of Francis I of France.

The book was composed, printed, and bound by American Book–Stratford Press, Inc., Saddle Brook, New Jersey. Typography and binding design by Cynthia Krupat.